As they neared the stable, Carole could hear the terrible whine of a siren. An ambulance pulled out of the driveway and turned toward the hospital, lights flashing, siren wailing. The diAngelo's Mercedes was parked carelessly in the lot, its doors left open.

But the only thing Carole really saw was the veterinarian's pickup truck and the county vet's wagon.

"Oh no!" she screamed, jumping from the car almost before it stopped. Lisa and Stevie came running out of the stable. Stevie had tears streaming down her face.

THE SADDLE CLUB

HORSE SHY

BONNIE BRYANT

A BANTAM SKYLARK BOOK®
NEW YORK · TORONTO · LONDON · SYDNEY · AUCKLAND

RL 5, 009-012

HORSE SHY

A Bantam Skylark Book / November 1988

Skylark Books is a registered trademark of Bantam Books,
a division of Bantam Doubleday Dell Publishing Group, Inc.
Registered in U.S. Patent and Trademark Office and elsewhere.

"The Saddle Club" is a trademark of Bonnie
Bryant Hiller. The Saddle Club design/logo, which
consists of an inverted U-shaped design, a riding crop,
and a riding hat, is a trademark of Bantam Books.

A special thanks to Miller's Harness Company for their help
in the preparation of the cover. Miller's clothing and accessories
are available through approved Miller's dealers throughout the
country. Address Miller's at 235 Murray Hill Parkway, East
Rutherford, New Jersey 07073 for further information.

ISBN 0-553-15611-X

Published simultaneously in the United States and Canada

*Bantam Books are published by Bantam Books, a division of Bantam
Doubleday Dell Publishing Group, Inc. Its trademark, consisting of the
words "Bantam Books" and the portrayal of a rooster, is Registered in U.S.
Patent and Trademark Office and in other countries. Marca Registrada.
Bantam Books, 1540 Broadway, New York, New York 10036.*

PRINTED IN THE UNITED STATES OF AMERICA

OPM   20 19 18 17 16 15 14 13 12 11

For my mother, Mary S. Bryant

"*DUCK!*" STEVIE LAKE yelled.

Lisa Atwood leaned forward in the saddle and tucked her head low, near Pepper's shiny black mane. She could feel tree branches brushing the back of her neck. When the brushing stopped, she sat upright and drew Pepper to a halt next to Stevie and her horse, Comanche. In a minute their friend, Carole Hanson, caught up with them, breathless and smiling, riding on Delilah.

"Oh, I love this trail!" Carole exclaimed. "But I do wish somebody would trim those branches! Sometimes when you're trotting, you come up on them so fast that you can ram right into them."

"Why don't the horses know to go around them?" Lisa asked her friends. Stevie and Carole were experienced riders. Lisa had begun riding just a few weeks earlier, but already she knew she loved the sport as much as anything she'd ever done.

"Horses don't go around the hanging branches because they can tell that they'll fit under them. They just forget about their riders on top," Carole explained.

"That's just the kind of thing you've got to know before we go on the overnight trail ride," Stevie said. "Riding outdoors is really different from riding indoors."

Lisa could already tell that was true. She'd been riding Pepper since her second lesson and she'd never known the horse to be so frisky.

"Okay, now we can trot here for a while before the trail gets rocky," Stevie said. "I'll start, you wait until I'm up to that azalea bush, and then you can follow." Stevie nudged Comanche into motion. As soon as Stevie passed the bright pink-flowered bush, Lisa signaled Pepper to trot. He obeyed immediately, following Comanche.

Lisa liked to trot. It was fast enough, but not too fast—sort of like jogging. A horse's next-fastest gait, the canter, was more like running, and Lisa found that scary sometimes; it was hard to keep her balance. While Pepper trotted, Lisa looked straight ahead, watching Stevie in front of her.

Stevie's untidy dark blond hair trailed out of her riding hat. The sun was shining on her hair and on Comanche's chestnut coat, making them both gleam richly. Their personalities, stubborn but playful, were alike. Somebody who didn't know Stevie well might think that the advantages she'd been born with—a comfortably wealthy family, big house, private schools—might have made her think she was better than other people. That wasn't Stevie at all. Stevie just liked to have fun, and she usually managed to do it, too—even when fun looked a lot like hot water!

Lisa glanced back at Carole. Carole was a wonderful rider. She'd been riding horses since she was a very little girl on the Marine Corps bases where her father had been stationed. Carole was riding Delilah, a beautiful, spirited palomino. Carole used her legs and reins to signal Delilah so subtly that Lisa could never even see what she'd done. But Delilah knew. The two worked in nearly perfect unison.

Lisa suddenly felt Pepper's trot quicken. She shortened her reins and slowed the horse a bit. They were approaching Stevie and Comanche. Stevie had slowed her horse to a walk to cool him down. Since the trail was wide, Lisa drew up next to Stevie and they walked together.

"How come Pepper started going faster when we got closer to you?"

"You've seen that happen in class, haven't you?" Lisa nodded. "Well," Stevie continued, "it happens more outdoors because there's more room. See, horses are naturally competitive animals. They really love to race and show off to each other. As soon as Pepper got close to Comanche, he wanted to be *ahead* of Comanche. It's not as important to him when we're walking as when we're trotting—and wait until you see what happens when we canter!"

"You know, Stevie, I've been wondering," Carole said as she drew her horse up to Comanche and Pepper. "Why was Max so eager to have us come out on the trail today?"

Max—whose full name was Maxmillian Regnery III and who was the owner of Pine Hollow Stables—was usually reluctant to let young riders onto the trails around the stable without a chaperon or instructor.

"Oh, he didn't know we were going on the trails," Stevie said airily. "I told him we were going to check the cross-country course for him."

"The cross-country course? You're crazy!" Carole told her.

"Oh, no, I'm not," Stevie countered. "There's going to be a horse show on that course this summer, so Max was really glad I wanted us to go over it. And, you'll remember that I'm supposed to be Lisa's partner on the Mountain Trail Overnight in three days, and if she doesn't have any trail experience before we leave, it'll be hard for her, and for me," Stevie finished breathlessly. "Now, I'm in the lead, so let's get going."

"But why didn't you just tell him the truth?" Carole asked. Stevie just shrugged and then began trotting again—as if that were an answer.

Lisa followed her, laughing a little bit to herself.

HORSE SHY 5

Stevie wasn't usually a bossy person the way she sounded now. What Stevie usually was was in trouble. Lisa had a sneaking suspicion that she'd be in it as well if she followed Stevie's orders. But how could she resist?

Carole watched the riders in front of her. She and Stevie had been riding together for two years, as long as her father had been stationed at the Marine Corps base at Quantico. Colonel Hanson had bought a house in nearby Willow Creek, Virginia—the first time they had ever lived off a base—and Carole had started riding at Pine Hollow. Until that time, most of her friends had been "military brats" like herself. Now, her best friends, Stevie and Lisa, were riders. The three of them had formed The Saddle Club. The only requirement for membership in it was to be horse crazy. So far, they hadn't met anybody as horse crazy as they were, so there were just the three members.

Even though Lisa was a year older than twelve-year-old Carole and Stevie, she'd just started riding. But Carole could tell that Lisa had a natural feel for horses. She'd known it the first time she'd watched Lisa ride in the ring at Pine Hollow. When Lisa and her mother had shown up at the stable, Carole was sure Lisa was just another spoiled rich kid, dressed in fancy riding clothes. Then Max had put her on a gentle pinto named Patch to see if she knew anything about horses. Before she'd walked around the ring twice, Veronica diAngelo (who really *was* a spoiled rich kid) had let a door slam loudly enough to frighten Lisa's horse. Patch had bolted into a gallop. Carole had been sure Lisa was going to fly off Patch's back and break an arm, or worse. Somehow, though, Lisa had managed to stay on the horse, eventually controlling him. Carole had never seen another rider show such skill the first time out. But no matter how great Lisa's natural talents were, there was plenty she didn't know. That's why this practice at riding outdoors was so important before the three girls went on the overnight ride.

Suddenly, Carole was alert. Delilah shied, nearly rearing, as a rabbit scooted across the trail. Carole leaned forward for balance, tightening the reins automatically. As soon as Delilah felt Carole's sure grip, she seemed to relax. The rabbit was safely in the underbrush by the time Delilah was calmed down.

Just then, a second rabbit dashed out onto the trail just in front of Pepper and Lisa. To Carole's horror, Pepper practically jumped backwards. Lisa grabbed the front of the saddle for balance, dropping Pepper's reins. Pepper reared a moment later, but without the reins, there was no way Lisa could control him or calm him. The rabbit darted back and forth under the horse's feet, completely terrorized. Pepper reared a second time, and when he landed, he took off—without Lisa. She flew into the air and landed on her right side.

Carole knew that Lisa needed help, but Pepper had

to be stopped. She called ahead to Stevie to help Lisa. When Stevie turned around and saw what had happened, she rushed to Lisa's aid.

Carole urged Delilah into action. Pepper had sprinted into the woods, but Carole knew there was a hilly field just beyond the stand of trees that bordered the trail. When she broke through the trees, she could see Pepper galloping up a hill. She had to cut him off before he could gallop down the hill—that could be really dangerous!

Skillfully, Carole directed Delilah. They took a shortcut across the pasture to meet Pepper at the hill's crest. Carole could almost feel Delilah shifting gears, thrilled with the race. They arrived at the hilltop just seconds before Pepper. Carole was afraid he might dart down the other side of the hill when he saw them in front of him, but he'd had enough of his run. Almost as if he knew he'd been naughty, he hung his head and coyly began nibbling at the sweet young grass in the pasture.

Carole clucked to him soothingly. He lifted his head and looked at her with his liquid brown eyes.

"It's okay, boy," she said. "Nobody's angry with you. We'd better see how Lisa feels, though. Come on."

He wouldn't come to her, but he stood patiently while she reached down from Delilah and took his reins. He followed obediently as they returned to the trail.

* * *

"YOU OKAY?" STEVIE asked. Lisa was still lying awkwardly on the ground.

"Well, I'm alive, if that's what you mean," Lisa said.

"No, I mean is anything broken or permanently damaged?"

"Yeah," Lisa said.

Stevie's heart fell. "What?" she asked.

"My dignity," Lisa told her grumpily.

Stevie laughed. "Boy, you had me scared! Come on, get up. Carole went after Pepper. There's a place by a brook about a half hour's ride ahead where we can stop and have our lunch. You'll feel better after you eat something."

"You ride; I'll walk," Lisa said.

"You *are* hurt!" Stevie said, offering Lisa a hand to stand up.

"No, I'm okay, but that's it for me for riding. I obviously can't do it. I'm quitting."

"Of course you can do it," Stevie said. "I mean, you could do it ten minutes ago—two minutes ago, actually."

"No, I couldn't," Lisa protested. "Look at what just happened."

"Just because your horse shies and you fall off, you think you can't ride?" Stevie asked her.

"You didn't fall off, did you?" Lisa answered her.

"Not then, maybe, but I have, plenty of times before. And I will again, too, believe me!"

Standing now, Lisa just glared at Stevie. Stevie returned the glare, looking carefully at Lisa. For one thing, she wanted to make sure she *was* okay, but for another, she was looking to see how scared she was. Lisa had taken a bad tumble and she was afraid she'd do it again. It was a feeling Stevie knew well; everybody who rode felt that way sometimes. But Stevie knew you couldn't let that get you down, and she certainly couldn't let it get one of her best friends down.

"Here's Pepper," Carole said cheerfully, leading him back through the stand of trees. "And I think he's ready to ride now."

"Well, his rider isn't," Lisa said.

Carole brought the horses to an abrupt halt.

"Lisa figures she's no good at riding," Stevie explained. "She's giving it up. Here and now." Stevie winked at Carole, certain she could rely on Carole to say just the right thing.

"I know how you feel, Lisa," Carole said. "It's rough when you decide to quit. But look at your poor horse." She pointed to Pepper. The horse's head still hung low. He glanced at Lisa quickly and then looked at the ground again. "He feels even worse than you do. Why don't you get back on him so he'll have the confidence to take riders again? If you abandon him now, who knows what will happen to him as a stable horse?"

Lisa looked Carole straight in the eye until she saw a twinkle there. "You're telling me to get right back up on the horse to make *him* feel better?" she asked.

When Carole shrugged in answer, Lisa giggled. "Maybe I'm being silly," she said, "but I can't help being scared."

"Don't worry," Carole said. "We understand. We've both felt the same way before. Now, forget how scary that fall was and climb up on this poor animal!"

Lisa brushed the dirt off her pants and removed some dry leaves from Pepper's saddle. She straightened out his bridle, which had gone askew, and she patted him on the neck.

"We're some pair, huh?" she said. "Come on now, boy, how can you be afraid of a little rabbit when I'm not allowed to be afraid of a great big horse?" She slid her left foot into the stirrup and lifted herself up into the saddle. "Oooh," she said. "Nothing's broken, but something's sure bruised. I may have to stand up to eat! How far is this picnic area?" she asked Stevie.

"Oh, not far," Stevie said vaguely as she urged Comanche on.

AN HOUR LATER, the three girls were finished with their picnic, and the horses were rested and refreshed from the cool brook water.

"We'd better get back to Pine Hollow," Stevie said. "Max isn't going to believe we spent three hours just looking at the cross-country course."

"Personally, I don't think Max is going to believe we even went to the cross-country course," Carole said. "He's smarter than that, you know."

Stevie already suspected Max knew what they were up to and approved. He trusted her as a rider, and he trusted Carole even more; he knew they'd take good care of Lisa.

"Listen, I've got a different way to go back," Stevie said. "It's through pastures. The horses will love it, too, because they can canter a lot. And when horses canter together outside, they usually end up galloping. Wait'll you try that, Lisa!"

"I think I've tried enough for today," Lisa said.

"Trust me," Stevie said with a grin. Somehow, the way she said it, Lisa trusted her, even though at the very same time, she suspected it was a mistake.

The girls took off on their horses through a series of pastures to return to Pine Hollow. Stevie seemed to know her way, and she was right about the horses enjoying the freedom of the pastures. They alternately walked, trotted, and cantered across the rolling hills. The only problem was that they had to stop all the time to open and close gates.

"It's an unbreakable rule of horseback riding that you leave gates exactly as you found them," Carole explained to Lisa.

"Hey, we can take a shortcut!" Stevie shouted.

"What shortcut?" Carole asked dubiously.

"Look over to the left." Stevie pointed downhill. "I'm sure that red building at the foot of the hill is next to Pine Hollow. If we go straight, we'll avoid about ten gates!"

"But we don't know whose farm that is!" Carole said. Another firm rule of riding was that riders only went where they had permission.

"Oh, who's going to care about three girls on horseback?" Stevie asked.

"A lot of people," Carole began to tell her, but it was too late. Stevie was already racing across the strange field, Lisa right behind. Carole sighed and followed them.

Lisa was enjoying the countryside, glad of her decision to ride Pepper again, and glad for the friends who made her do it.

The girls were about three quarters of the way across the field when they heard a strange sound.

At first, Lisa didn't know what it was. It sounded a little bit like a cow. But there weren't any cows in this small pasture. Herds of cows usually grazed together.

When she saw it, she knew it wasn't a cow, but she wished it were! A very large bull emerged from behind a stand of aspens. He snorted and bellowed, stomping at the ground with one front foot. His nostrils flared in anger. Lisa drew in her reins. All three girls began walking their horses slowly, hoping the bull would let them pass.

All at once, though, he began charging. He was perhaps fifty yards from the horses, and although his legs were short and he was stocky, he was fast. Very fast.

"Get out of here!" Stevie hollered, turning Comanche around and heading for the fence. Delilah and Pepper took off as well. Then, in horror, Lisa realized that there was no gate there! They'd be cornered! A rabbit was one thing for Pepper to contend with, but a bull? Before Lisa could figure out what the answer was, Stevie showed her. As soon as Comanche got close to the fence, Stevie leaned forward, rising in the seat. Then Comanche was airborne, lifting himself gracefully over the fence, landing smoothly on the other side. Stevie cantered on a few steps and then drew her horse to a halt, waiting for her friends.

Carole, on board Delilah, cleared the fence with a foot to spare. It looked so easy!

Terrified, Lisa rose in the saddle as she'd seen her friends do. She leaned forward, grabbing some of Pepper's mane in her sweaty hands. Just when she was afraid they would crash headfirst into the wooden fence, her friends cried "Now!" Maybe Pepper heard them. Maybe he just knew what he was supposed to do. It didn't matter to Lisa how it happened, because it happened. While she clutched the saddle and mane with all her strength, she felt Pepper lift off the ground and sail to safety on the other side of the fence.

Lisa had never been more thrilled—or more scared—in her life. Stevie and Carole cheered wildly, clapping for Pepper and for Lisa.

"Gee, I didn't know you could jump!" Stevie said.

"Neither did I," Lisa said. "Neither did I."

"IF ONE MORE person asks me where the extra stirrup leathers are, I'm going to scream!" Carole announced. But nobody was listening to her.

Everything around the stable and front driveway of Pine Hollow Stables was in an advanced state of confusion. It seemed to Carole that she was the only organized part of it.

The eleven people and eleven horses who were going on the Mountain Trail Overnight—or the MTO, as the girls called it—were swarming around the bus and horse vans. All the riders were trying to make sure their own things were packed. Carole clutched a clipboard tightly in her hand. She checked it one more time—a *final* time, she hoped—but she knew better.

"Need any help?" Stevie asked, hauling her own bedroll and knapsack over to the bus.

"Hey, thanks," Carole said. "Everybody else wants to know how I can help *them*." Carole looked at the clipboard again. "Oh, here's what you can do. We're going to need hoof-picks. Joe Novick said he'd get them, but right after he promised, I saw him go in the opposite direction and I haven't seen him since. Grab a couple from the tack room, will you? And put them in with the grooming gear?"

Stevie saluted with a grin and headed for the stable's tack room. Carole put a second check mark next to "hoof-picks."

Veronica diAngelo was standing near the bus. Three of her friends—more like ladies-in-waiting, Carole thought—were gathered around her. Carole stifled a giggle when she noticed that each of them—Meg Durham, Lorraine Olsen, and Betsy Cavanaugh—was wearing the identical riding pants that Veronica had worn. Last week. They'd probably driven their mothers crazy trying to imitate Veronica's fashion-show riding habit.

As far as Carole was concerned, there was nothing about Veronica that she wanted to imitate—but Veronica did have one thing Carole longed for. Veronica's father had bought her a beautiful Thoroughbred stallion named Cobalt. Carole would have given anything to own Cobalt, and sometimes it almost seemed like she did. Veronica liked owning a prize Thoroughbred.

She didn't like taking care of him and exercising him regularly, though. She often asked Carole to help and Carole never said no. She loved that horse.

"Did we remember to bring horse blankets?" Red O'Malley, one of Pine Hollow's stableboys, asked Carole.

She checked her list and told him they were packed.

When Carole was certain everything on her clipboard had been checked twice, she helped load the horses onto the vans. Most horses learned to accept occasional van trips. Some even liked them. But a few, like Barq, whom Lorraine would ride, were van haters. He was an Arabian—named after the Arabic word for lightning—and when he got near a van, he tried to streak the other way! To avoid trouble this time, they led him up the ramp with a bucket of oats. With his nose in the feed bag, he was in the van before he knew it, and it was too late for protests.

Today, Carole saw with a sigh of relief, Barq was no trouble at all. Diablo and Harry gave Max and Red a hard time, but eventually, the horses were loaded. When Carole assured the drivers that all the horse gear was aboard, the vans took off. The bus would follow in a few minutes.

Lisa stowed her bedroll and pack in the bus and came over to chat with Carole while the last items were loaded. She was followed closely by her mother. Mrs. Atwood had originally insisted that Lisa learn to ride. She thought all nice young ladies should know something about horses. But she never expected Lisa to become horse crazy, and she was very nervous that something terrible would happen to her daughter on the MTO.

She hovered around Lisa. While the girls talked about riding, Mrs. Atwood uttered dire warnings like "Don't go too close to the edge of the mountain, now, dear," and "Don't drink any water that hasn't been boiled, will you?" Lisa just nodded sweetly, assuring her mother she'd be careful. Carole wondered at Lisa's patience, but she knew Mrs. Atwood was just being caring, in her own way.

"Mom, I think it's time for parents to go," Lisa said gently. She gave her mother a brief hug. "See you Sunday at six o'clock, okay?"

"Okay, dear," Mrs. Atwood said, backing toward her station wagon. "Have a good time!" Lisa smiled.

Lisa wasn't the only rider with a mother hanging around. Mrs. diAngelo drove up in her Mercedes and rolled down the window. "Oh, I'm so glad you're still here, dear," she said. "I brought this for you."

Mrs. diAngelo offered Veronica a set of saddlebags. Even from across the parking area, Carole could see they weren't just saddlebags. They were from Hermès, the exclusive French saddlery. Carole knew she'd probably ridden horses that cost less than that set of saddlebags.

Veronica accepted the offering as if her mother had handed her an old pair of pajamas. "Thanks, Mother," she said drily.

"Open them up," her mother said, her voice tinged with excitement. Veronica lifted up the flap and pulled out a sack of expensive Perugina candies. "I thought you'd enjoy sharing those by the campfire," she said.

Veronica smiled briefly. "Thanks, Mother. I guess it's time to go now. See you Sunday."

Mrs. diAngelo raised her push-button window and drove off.

"Isn't that something?" Stevie said, joining Carole and Lisa. "I didn't know she cared."

Carole had to agree. Mrs. diAngelo seemed to be trying very hard to please Veronica. It was too bad that Veronica was such a pain. "Doesn't matter to me, though," Carole said. "She's still a pain."

"Yeah, but now she's a pain with some wonderful treats to share at the campfire."

"You know," Lisa said, "I think I'd rather have a mother who worries too much than one who brings me five-hundred-dollar saddlebags filled with expensive candies."

"Me, too," Stevie agreed.

Carole was quiet for a moment. Her own mother had died after a long illness the previous fall. She hadn't been like either Mrs. Atwood or Mrs. diAngelo. She'd been just about perfect. Carole really missed her, but she was glad she had her memories.

"Time to board the bus!" Max announced. At once, eleven people jostled over to the minibus, which would carry them to the start of the mountain trail.

Carole stood at the door of the bus. As the riders climbed aboard one by one, Carole asked them all—even Max—if they'd remembered their bedrolls and packs. As they promised they had, Carole put checks by their names on her list.

Then it was time for Carole to climb on board. "Okay, Hanson, did you remember *your* bedroll and backpack?" Stevie teased, trying to sound like a Marine drill instructor.

Carole blushed. She knew then that she'd been impossibly bossy, but there were so many things to do, and Max was really counting on her to help.

"Of course!" she answered. She could envision the two bundles clearly. Right by her front door. Ready to be picked up and put in the car. She gasped. She knew suddenly that they were still there, right by her front door. If she didn't have her pack and bedroll, there was no way she could go on the trip! Max would probably agree to take a detour past her house to pick them up, but could she ever live it down?

She stood, frozen, on the steps of the bus. Then she heard the sound of a car horn. Startled, she turned around. Her father! He pulled up in front of the bus, then threw open the door and dragged out the two bundles Carole most wanted to see.

"Didn't think you'd want to go without these, honey," he said, handing them to Carole. She slung them into the luggage compartment and slammed its door shut.

"Thanks, Daddy," she said. And then, while everybody watched and waited, she gave him the great big hug he deserved. "You're the best."

"Yeah, I know," he told her. "You have a good time, hear?" She smiled at him.

"Hey, Colonel Hanson!" Stevie hollered out the bus window. The colonel waved a greeting to her. They were great friends, constantly trading old jokes with each other. "What has four legs and a trunk?" Stevie asked.

"An elephant going on a trip," he shot back.

"And what do you call Carole when *she* goes on a trip?" Stevie asked.

"Forgetful!" he said. When everybody was done laughing, Carole boarded the bus.

And they were off!

CAROLE COULDN'T BELIEVE it, but getting everything *un*loaded at the start of the trail was almost as much trouble as getting it loaded.

Delilah was unusually docile coming off the trailer, but it turned out that Barq hated getting off as much as he hated getting on. Red O'Malley got a nasty kick on his shin. He grimaced, but said it was okay. Carole thought it would be swollen and black-and-blue for a long time. Horses were big animals, and strong. If you were going to spend a lot of time with them, you had to be prepared to get hurt some of the time. Red didn't complain; he knew that, too.

Finally, the horses were unloaded, and the camping and picnic gear was loaded onto a van that would meet them at the rendezvous for lunch and then the overnight campsite.

"I hope the truck doesn't get lost," Carole joked with Lisa and Stevie.

When their horses were all off the van, the riders each fetched tack and began saddling.

"I always hate tacking up—especially when Comanche's in a bad mood," Stevie said. "But Comanche's standing still today. I think he's as eager to get going as I am!"

"I think you're right," Lisa said. "Look at Pepper. He's so busy sniffing the fresh mountain air that he didn't even notice when I tightened the girth!" Pepper had a way of taking in a big breath of air when his rider drew the girth tight. Then, after it had been fastened, he'd let out his breath and his saddle would be nice and loose, the way he liked it. From his rider's point of view, though, it was dangerous. Lisa always had to tighten the girth twice. This time, though, it wasn't necessary.

"Mount up!" Max called, and the trail ride really began.

MAX HAD TOLD the riders that their first day would be relatively easy. They would ride for an hour or so to their picnic lunch rendezvous. Then, after lunch, they would be going uphill most of the way to a meadow about halfway up the mountain. They were supposed to reach the meadow by midafternoon. The horses would spend the night in the meadow, and the campsite was just uphill from it.

Lisa couldn't believe how lucky she was. Just a month ago, she'd never ridden anything more exciting than a pony in a zoo. Now, here she was on a warm, sparkling day, riding through a beautiful mountain forest just bursting with late-spring flowers. They rode single file on the narrow path, shaded by majestic oak trees. For the first half mile, the way was lined with mountain laurel, covered with pink and white blossoms. Lisa picked a small flower and tucked it behind her ear. It made her feel exotic.

"Can you believe this place?" Stevie asked from behind her.

"No, I can't," Lisa said. "It makes me feel like I'm in a dream, or maybe a fairy tale. I sort of expect to see a little gingerbread cottage around the next bend."

Just then the trail widened in a hemlock grove. The warm sunshine seemed to bake the trees and the carpet of pine needles. There was a wonderful forest smell all around them.

"Doesn't it smell like Christmas?" Carole called back to her friends. She inhaled deeply, thinking how great the fresh evergreen scent was.

While the trail was wide, Max had the group trot and then canter, one at a time. Pepper was ready. He was frisky and full of excitement. Lisa thought maybe he was as excited as she was. She'd never known him so eager to respond to her signals. When she sat in the trot and then nudged him behind his girth with her left leg, he responded immediately, springing into a wonderful rocking canter. It had never felt so good. It had never been so much fun. She tucked her head down behind Pepper's to avoid some low-slung hemlock branches. As she reined him back down to a walk where the path narrowed again, she sighed contentedly.

"Did you like that?" Stevie asked.

"It was *wonderful*," she replied truthfully. She couldn't stop grinning, and she felt that in his own way Pepper was grinning, too.

"I'M SO HUNGRY, I could eat a—" Stevie paused. "Elephant," she said, giggling.

Lisa groaned at Stevie's joke. "I think I'll make do with the peanut butter sandwiches I saw Mrs. Reg making this morning," she said, referring to Max's mother who was well-loved by the girls.

"We'll eat soon enough," Carole told her friends. "But we'd better see to the horses first."

Lisa and Stevie obediently followed Carole to the area where the horses were tied up.

The three girls took their heavy-duty buckets to the creek and scooped the fresh, cool water for their horses.

"Not too much," Carole warned Lisa.

"That's right, you never want to give a hot horse a lot of water to drink at once," Stevie explained. "They can get terrible stomach cramps that way. Same thing can happen to people, you know."

"Yeah, I know," Lisa said. "After ballet class they only let us have sips of water, especially on hot days." Considering how heavy the bucket could be when it was full, Lisa was relieved she only had to fill it a quarter full. Pepper was glad for the water and nuzzled her neck when she brought the bucket. When he'd had a few sips, she gave him a handful of hay from the bale the van had brought. Pepper seemed totally content. Lisa and Stevie returned to the picnic area, promising to save a spot for Carole.

Carole watched Delilah drinking and patted the golden horse's neck softly. Delilah's mood seemed changed. The horse was enjoying herself, but she was more reserved than usual. She'd been happy to follow Carole's directions, but somehow the usual fight in her seemed faded. Carole supposed she should have been happy with that change, but any mood change in a horse could signal trouble. She made a mental note to talk with Max about it.

When Delilah was munching on her hay, Carole knew it was time for her PBJ and fruit punch. She was hungry and ready for them. She returned to the picnic site, grabbed two sandwiches, some carrot sticks, and a mug of juice, and looked around for Lisa and Stevie. They had just sat down under a big old hickory tree, which was surrounded by soft green ferns.

"Having a good time?" Betsy Cavanaugh asked Carole as she passed. Betsy was sitting with Veronica and the rest of her fan club.

"I sure am. How about you?"

"Oh, it's wonderful," Betsy said.

Carole smiled in acknowledgment and began to walk on. But something made her look back at Veronica, who was sitting on a rock with an empty plate and mug at her side. She had her boots off and was completely relaxed.

If Veronica was already finished with her lunch, that could only mean that she hadn't done anything about Cobalt. Carole knew that, once again, Veronica had just assumed that somebody would do her work for her. And once again, she was right. *She doesn't deserve that horse*, Carole told herself, taking her plate over to the hickory tree.

"Keep the ants out of my lunch for a few minutes, will you?" she asked her friends.

"Sure," Lisa agreed, tucking a napkin over the sandwiches.

Carole returned to the horse area. It only took a few minutes to give Cobalt some water and hay. She knew she should have made Veronica do it herself, but Carole got tremendous pleasure from everything she did with this majestic horse. She patted his sleek neck after she fed him, and he nickered with pleasure.

When she was sure he was properly fed and watered, she returned for her own lunch.

MIRACULOUSLY, THEY ARRIVED at their meadowside campsite a full half hour ahead of schedule.

"Can you believe this?" Stevie asked Carole. "We're actually early!"

"Yeah, it's great," Carole agreed. "The horses all practically pranced through the last couple of miles of trails. I guess they're glad for the chance for a good run."

"You mean they're having as much fun as we are!" Stevie teased.

Max told the boys and girls to tie up their horses outside the paddock where the horses would be penned for the night and to keep the saddles on them.

"The horses should cool down a bit and relax while we set up the campsite. Then, when we're all finished with that, I want to play some horse games. Is that okay with you all?" he asked.

He didn't have to ask twice! Carole knew that horse games were some of the most fun of all.

"ALL RIGHT," MAX told his riders a half hour later. "We're going to play a game called Around the World. There are two teams, five each, and each member is assigned a number, one to five. We make a large circle in no particular order. I'll call out a number and a pace, for example, 'Number Ones, trot.' Then, the two 'Number One' riders will trot around the circle to their right, and whoever gets back to their original position first wins a point for the team. If you break gait—either faster or slower—or go back to the wrong spot, the other rider in your pair wins a point and a point is deducted from your team's total."

"Oh, boy, this is going to be fun. I hope we get the boys on our team," Stevie said. "I certainly don't want Veronica and her shadows!" She'd seen Veronica play games before and she knew she was an incredibly bad sport.

"I have the funny feeling it's not going to work that way," Carole warned her. Much to Stevie's dismay, The Saddle Club was broken up. She and Carole were on one team, with Meg, Lorraine, and Red. Lisa was teamed up with Veronica, Joe, Betsy, and Adam Levine, one of Max's newer students. Stevie saw Lisa grimace when Max announced the teams. But she could tell that Max was trying to match skill levels on the teams.

Soon the numbers were assigned and they all formed a circle. Max and his horse, Diablo, stood in the center of the ring as Max hollered out numbers and gaits. Stevie waited anxiously for her number—three—to be called. And then it was.

"Number Threes, canter!" Max cried.

Stevie was surprised to find herself competing with Lisa. The teams had kept their number assignments secret. Lisa was such a new rider that Stevie was sure she would beat her. But Lisa pulled Pepper out of the circle and turned him to the right very quickly. He broke into a canter, and before Stevie had circled the ring, Lisa and Pepper were breathlessly pulling back into their spot.

Stevie laughed and waved at Lisa. She'd been so cocksure of herself that she hadn't even tried too hard. Lisa had won, fair and square, and she'd deserved to win. *This* time.

When the first game ended, Stevie's team, the Blues, had won, in spite of her own carelessness. In the second game, it seemed that the Reds had learned their lesson and tried much harder. The final score was close—three to two—but the Reds were victors.

"Final match!" Max announced. "Losers will collect kindling for the fire!"

It was just like Max to assign jobs by horsemanship. Usually Stevie wouldn't mind doing something like collecting kindling, but she certainly didn't want to do it if it meant that somebody had beat her at something! She glanced around at her teammates. As usual, Carole's calm, assured face revealed nothing. But Carole was matched against Adam Levine and she was eight times the rider he was. She had beat him twice. Everybody knew she'd beat him a third time.

Stevie saw the looks of determination on the faces of Meg, Lorraine, and Red. She was pretty sure they'd win.

"Number Fours, trot!" Max called to start off the final game. Lorraine and Betsy took off. It wasn't even close. Lorraine's horse didn't want to trot at all. Betsy won easily. The Reds were ahead, one to nothing.

"Number Fives, walk!" Max announced.

Red and Joe took off at a stately walk. Joe was an okay rider, but Red was better. He knew how to urge his horse, Harry, into an extended walk. Harry and Red won easily.

When Carole and Adam had to trot, it was the same story. Carole knew how to get Delilah to lengthen her strides so that, with each beat, she covered more ground. Adam got Tecumseh to a nice collected trot, but it wasn't enough and Carole won easily.

"Number Twos, canter!" Veronica and Meg were off in an instant, but not before Stevie saw the bratty look on Veronica's face. Veronica had never been particularly competitive, but Stevie suspected she'd rather do almost anything than collect twigs. And she did. While Veronica was behind Max's back, she urged Cobalt from a canter to a gallop, which was a much faster gait. Veronica would win easily. Stevie saw Meg glance across the circle. The open-mouthed look on Meg's face revealed that she'd seen Veronica break her gait. But then Meg's mouth closed into a thin line of determination. Stevie knew that if Meg tattled on Veronica, she'd be banned from Veronica's circle of friends forever. That was not a price Meg would be willing to pay.

For her own part, Stevie wasn't interested in tattling. If Max hadn't seen the gallop, well, Stevie and the Blues would take their chances. The score was tied.

Before Max called the final pair, Stevie had a moment to wonder who else had seen what Veronica had done. Maybe someone would say something after the game.

"Number Threes, trot!" Stevie and Lisa turned their horses out of the circle. Stevie nudged Comanche with her heels and he broke into a good extended trot. But when Stevie glanced across the circle it was clear that Pepper, still inspired by the great outdoors, was trotting very quickly and was beating Comanche. Stevie wanted to win—*really* wanted to win. She urged Comanche ahead and he responded with a longer stride, but Stevie wasn't at all sure it would be enough.

Every competitor knows that it's usually an awful mistake to look at your competition in a race, but Stevie kept watching Lisa. She was doing really well and Stevie couldn't help being a little proud of her. After all, who had helped her since she'd started riding!

While Stevie stole peeks at Lisa and Pepper, she saw, to her astonishment, that Lisa was pulling in on Pepper's reins. It wasn't easy to see, but she definitely moved them toward her hips. In an instant, Pepper drew to a walk. He broke his gait! That automatically meant victory for the Blues! Stevie completed her circle, pulled Comanche back into her place in the circle, and waited for Lisa to finish her round.

As Stevie watched, she expected to see embarrassment on Lisa's face. After all, breaking from a trot to a walk was really baby stuff. Lisa was better than that. But when Stevie looked at Lisa's face, what she saw instead was a sly smile, and then she understood.

Lisa had seen Veronica's stunt. If she'd tattled, it might have ruined the whole camp-out. So she'd done the only thing that would guarantee the right outcome of the game. She'd thrown it. She had intentionally pulled Pepper into a walk. Everybody would believe it was just a mistake since that was the kind of thing that happened to new riders.

Stevie was proud of the way Lisa had handled the situation. She wondered if she'd have had the guts to do the same thing.

"How could you *do* that?" Veronica wailed at Lisa.

"I dunno," Lisa said dumbly.

"Well, you're not going to be on *my* team again! Ever!" Veronica declared.

"*Fine* by me," Lisa said.

Stevie grinned over at Carole.

4

"CAROLE, SOMETIMES I wonder what I'd do without you," Max said.

Carole beamed. Max wasn't the kind of man who complimented people easily. In fact, he hadn't said anything nice about her riding until the third class she'd taken with him!

"I like to help," she said, straightening Patch's blanket and retying the strings at his neck. It was always cool in the mountains at night and the horses would be glad for the covers. "Besides, if I'm ever actually going to own a horse farm, I'll have to get used to the work."

"And it's a *lot* of work," Max assured her.

"It's a lot more work than it ought to be if you've got somebody like Veronica boarding her horse with you," Red said, as Max walked away to check Diablo's blanket. The disgust in his voice was clear. "She didn't even bother with grain for Cobalt's dinner—"

"I'll take care of that," Carole said eagerly.

"I did it already," Red said. "I thought you did your part at lunch."

Carole wasn't surprised that Red had also noticed Veronica's carelessness at lunchtime.

"These are really barn horses," Max told Carole when he returned. "They need extra special care when they are on the trail."

That reminded Carole of something she'd been meaning to ask him. "Gosh, Max, speaking of that, Delilah's been acting strangely. Could she be sick, do you think?"

"What do you mean?" Max snapped, instantly concerned.

"It's like she's suddenly sort of ladylike, more gentle than usual. But, then, she tried to bite me when I was feeding her tonight. She just seems unpredictable."

Max laughed. "Women," he said. "It doesn't sound to me like there's anything to worry about."

But Carole still wasn't sure.

STEVIE LEANED AGAINST a tree, scratching her tired back on its rough bark. The day had been great, and now she knew they were about to play one of the students' favorite games. It was informally called Who Was Max the First?

Maxmillian Regnery III was the current owner and operator of Pine Hollow Stables. It had been founded by his grandfather early in the century. Some people around town remembered Max's father, known as Max the Second. He was a stern, sour-faced man, known for strutting along the town's sidewalks, slapping a riding crop into the palm of his hand. Max the First had died more than 50 years earlier and it had become a Pine Hollow tradition to sort through the wild stories about what kind of man would establish such a wonderful place as Pine Hollow.

"He was a Rough Rider, you know," Stevie began.

"I always thought Max the First was a *good* rider," Meg protested.

"No, I mean a Rough Rider, like pounding up San Juan Hill with Teddy Roosevelt and the Rough Riders. Remember that stuff about the Spanish-American War?"

"Oh, yeah," Meg said. "Roosevelt was the guy who said 'Speak softly and carry a big stick'?"

"That's right!" Stevie said. "And that's why Max the Second always carried his riding crop in town!"

Everybody laughed, except Joe Novick. He was waiting for a quiet moment. "I don't think so," he said. The crowd around the campfire turned to hear *his* theory. "I mean, well, maybe he did that *before* . . ."

"Before *what?*" Betsy Cavanaugh asked eagerly.

"Well, the earthquake, of course," Joe said matter-of-factly. "See, the way I figure it, he was in San Francisco in 1906. You know those old sand buckets in the stables?" They all knew them. Fire was a constant threat in a stable and, in addition to the standard fire extinguishers, there were old leather sand buckets every few feet. "I think he was part of the horseback bucket brigade that saved the city of San Francisco—"

"Saved it?" Carole interrupted. "The whole place was burned down!"

"I just thought the buckets were mementos of the Great Fire," Joe finished.

Maybe they were.

"Oh, no, no," Lisa jumped in, entering into the spirit of the thing. "You've got this all wrong." Everybody turned to her. Even Max seemed interested in what she had to say. "A name like Maxmillian Regnery has to be a cover," she began. "I just learned in school that the Latin word for king is *rex* or *regis,* so the name *Regnery* was chosen because Max the First had royal blood, and I think it was Russian royal blood!"

The kids around the campfire burst into laughter. This was the strangest theory yet. While they listened, Lisa explained that Max the First was probably actually a son of the Russian czar Nicholas II. "He and Alexandra had so many kids, nobody could keep track of them. And when the revolution began, Max the First began spying for the revolutionaries. That's how he escaped execution. But he was always afraid the royalists would find him. So he escaped to Virginia, changed his name, and opened Pine Hollow!"

There was a great round of applause for Lisa's new, untested theory.

"Not bad," Stevie told her, grinning with amusement. At school, Lisa was a straight-A student. Now Stevie could see some use for all the knowledge Lisa had to acquire to be so good.

Adam Levine took Lisa's story about Russian history as a challenge.

"I think you're on the completely wrong track," he began, trying not to laugh. "You're ignoring the well-known fact that Mrs. Reg always keeps that broom near her desk. It was, of course, the broom Max the First's mother used to fly on Halloween. She wouldn't let *him* fly it, so he started riding horses."

Everybody burst into laughter.

"Come on, Max," Meg urged. "What's the real truth?"

The campers turned to him and waited. Max never commented on the silly stories about his grandfather, which, of course, just made the old man seem all the more mysterious. "Well, I'll tell you this," he said, and then paused. Stevie wondered if he might actually reveal something of the truth. A cricket chirped. When the last chirp had echoed in the darkness, Max continued. "I'll tell you this," he repeated. "I think you're on the right track now."

He'd sounded so serious that, for a moment, Stevie had believed him.

Later on, tucked into sleeping bags, safe in their tent, Lisa and Stevie giggled about the silly stories. Carole, tired and happy, plopped a pillow over her ears and went to sleep immediately.

"You know, there is a true answer to the question about Max the First," Lisa whispered to Stevie so she wouldn't wake Carole up.

"Sure, I know that, but there have been so many outrageous rumors that there's no way to tell the truth anymore!"

"Well, we could go back to the beginning," Lisa suggested.

"You mean travel through time?"

"No, I mean go to the library and look through the town records. The man lived in Willow Creek. He bought land, he had children. We ought to be able to find out *something* about him with a little research."

Lisa, the straight-A student, was coming through again. "That's a great idea!" Stevie said. "And I bet when we find out the truth, nobody will believe us."

"Sure, everybody knows that truth is stranger than fiction."

What a delicious idea that was. Stevie snuggled down and closed her eyes. She went to sleep dreaming of Max the First, tied to the mast of a pirate ship.

THE NEXT MORNING, Lisa sat on Pepper next to Max and Diablo. They were both watching the other students doing a combination jump—first over a brook, and then, a few yards farther on, over a log that lay across the forest path.

"These aren't hard jumps," Max told Lisa when Betsy Cavanaugh had cleared the log on Patch. "But you're not ready to start jumping classes. You may begin jump classes twelve months after you start your regular riding classes. Perhaps next year you could try a jump like this."

Lisa just nodded. There was no *way* she was going to tell Max she'd already jumped a four-foot fence! Max was very strict about what his students learned and when they learned it. Nobody, but nobody, began jumping until she'd been riding for at least a year. For now, Lisa had to be satisfied to watch the others.

She didn't mind a bit. Nothing could bother Lisa today. She was having such a wonderful time on the trip that even a thunderstorm wouldn't dampen her spirits. She was loving every minute. Take this morning, for instance. Lisa had awakened early. She'd crawled out of her sleeping bag and, curious to watch the horses at play, she'd walked down to the paddock near the campsite.

The sight that had greeted her was beautiful almost beyond her own imagination. In the pasture, hazy with morning mists, were eleven horses and seven deer! The deer had obviously jumped the fences, probably to eat some of the oats the horses might have missed. Lisa had held her breath. She'd been afraid that if she breathed, it would all go away, as if it were a dream.

In a moment it had gone away. From the campsite, Lisa heard a bloodcurdling shriek—unmistakably Veronica diAngelo. The second her voice pierced the silence, the deer fled, soaring over the fences. When Lisa had returned to the campsite, she learned that Veronica had discovered a daddy longlegs spider near her sleeping bag. Lisa knew they were completely harmless and was annoyed with Veronica. She had wanted to share the beautiful sight with The Saddle Club—and Veronica, true to form, had ruined it.

"Lean forward, Joe! Rise in the saddle . . . NOW!" Max called. Lisa turned her attention back to the jumping. At that instant, Dusty flew into the air over the creek. He landed smoothly, took another three strides, and then rose over the log. It was great to watch, and Lisa could really learn while she did it.

"He's got a good jump position," Max confided to her. "Keep a mental picture of it for yourself. For when the time comes, I mean."

"Okay," she assured him. "He was holding Dusty's mane. Is that a good idea?" she asked.

"Can't talk now," Max shushed her. "Here comes Veronica."

Veronica and Cobalt came galloping down the path toward the creek.

"Slow down to a canter!" Max yelled.

But Veronica didn't pull Cobalt back at all. In fact, to Lisa's eye, she seemed to rush her horse even more. Cobalt was going very fast as he neared the creek. Veronica rose in the saddle and nudged him to jump. His sleek body lifted into the air and landed on the far side of the creek. But he was off-balance. Cobalt stumbled. Veronica whacked him with her riding crop. He righted himself and took another two strides before jumping the small log. His next landing was smoother, but only a little bit.

"Veronica, come over here!" Max commanded.

Veronica's face was set with a look that said "you can't tell me anything." But she waited impatiently while Max spoke to her.

"You *are* aware that you cannot gallop a horse up to a jump like that? You *must* slow down before you jump! The horse's body has far too much weight in the front to be able to fling himself over a jump the way you expect Cobalt to be able to do it. If you care for your horse, you will not do that again."

"Yes, Max," she said, without the slightest tinge of regret in her voice. She signaled Cobalt into motion and turned him around to join the advancing riders.

Max shook his head slightly, angrily. Then, when he realized that Stevie was about to jump, he turned all his attention to her.

Lisa watched Stevie as well, but her thoughts were on Veronica. She thought Max must have enjoyed giving Veronica a lecture. After all, she was the daughter of the richest man in town—a banker who held the mortgage on Pine Hollow Stables. Veronica was a total pain, but Lisa and everybody else knew that Max had to put up with her.

"WHERE DID YOU disappear to so early this morning?" Carole asked Lisa later. The three girls were helping Red water the horses and give them lunch before their own picnic.

"It was the deer!" Lisa said, almost breathlessly. This was the first chance there had been all day for The Saddle Club members to talk. Carole and Stevie listened intently as Lisa described the scene in the pasture at dawn.

"I thought I saw some deer along the trail yesterday afternoon. But to see them grazing with the horses! That must have been outstanding!" Stevie said.

"It was," Lisa said. "Want to get up early tomorrow and see if it happens again?"

"You bet!" Carole and Stevie agreed.

"Just hope Miss Perfect diAngelo doesn't scare them away again," Stevie said.

"Oh, I don't think she'll be scaring anything," Lisa said. "Not after the bawling out Max gave her."

"About what?" Stevie asked, wickedly interested.

"About galloping Cobalt down to the jump," Lisa explained. "I think he was just having a good time because he had a good excuse to yell at her. I mean, nothing happened to her or Cobalt."

"You're kidding!" Stevie said.

"No, he really told her off," Lisa said.

"I'm sure he did!" Carole said. "Did she really gallop down that hill to the jump?"

"Uh-huh," Lisa said. "What's the big deal?"

"You're such a good rider that sometimes I forget you don't know much," Stevie said.

"Thanks," Lisa said stiffly.

"I'm sorry—that came out the wrong way," Stevie said, realizing she'd hurt Lisa's feelings. "That's a compliment." Lisa looked at her sideways. "What I meant," Stevie went on, "was that you're really a good rider, even though you're so new at it!"

Lisa nodded. "That's okay," she said.

"Well, you know the old joke about how a camel is supposed to be a horse—designed by a committee?"

Lisa smiled. Stevie was famous for telling "old" jokes. She'd heard that one. It meant that when a lot of people get together to accomplish something one person *should* do alone, the results are often goofed-up.

"See," Stevie continued seriously, "in some ways, a horse *is* a horse designed by a committee." Lisa cocked her head to listen carefully. Stevie and Carole knew so much about horses!

"A horse has two sets of legs: the big, strong ones in the back where most of the power comes from— that's the good part of the design—and then there are the weaker legs in the front. The problem is that almost two thirds of a horse's weight is carried by his front legs. Now, when the back legs push off *really* hard like they do when the horse is galloping—*especially* downhill—then when the horse lands out of a jump, his weaker front legs take one heck of a beating. And sometimes they don't make it. The horse can stumble and fall, he can throw the rider—all kinds of things can happen. Veronica should know better."

"I didn't realize it was that serious," Lisa said.

"It is," Carole told her. "Poor baby."

Carole turned to Cobalt, and gave the big black horse a hug. He nodded, as if to hug her back, and then nickered gently, nuzzling her ear.

"I think they're in love," Stevie told Lisa, joking. But as both girls watched, each knew that it wasn't really a joking matter.

"Now, we're going to canter in jump position," Max announced to the group. "One at a time. Carole, you begin."

One by one, the students rose out of their saddles, putting all their weight on their stirrups. Lisa lifted herself up and leaned forward the way Carole had done. Max had had her practice this position since her second lesson. It was important for learning balance, and balance was important for riding.

Pepper picked up a trot, and when his gait was rhythmic and steady, she touched his belly behind the girth with her left heel. He immediately began shifting into a canter. Twenty yards ahead of her, Stevie was doing the same thing. Almost as soon as she began cantering, Lisa got the feeling that something was wrong. First, Pepper's ears began twitching every which way, then they laid back, almost flat to his head—a very bad sign. He was listening for trouble.

Then Lisa could hear it, too. Another horse was coming up close behind her. Pepper was usually even-tempered, except when there was a horse right at his flank. If Lisa tried to slow him down, the other horse would get closer. If she tried to speed him up, she'd be in worse trouble!

"Pepper," she whispered. "It's okay—just keep going. There, there, boy." The words sounded calming to her, but Pepper wasn't in the mood for them. His ears twitched some more. Although the path was nice and wide, Pepper shifted over to the extreme right side, perhaps trying to cut off the horse behind him. Lisa glanced over her right shoulder to see who was there. Just at that moment, Pepper shifted over to the left side of the trail. If she'd been seated and balanced, it would have been no trouble, but Lisa was too far out of her saddle and her balance had been upset when she looked over her shoulder. Pepper went over to the left, all right, but Lisa stayed on the right side of the path—in the weeds!

As she tumbled off Pepper, she rolled forward, landing harmlessly on her shoulder. As soon as she landed, Pepper drew to a halt across the path. He looked at her, seeming surprised to find her on the ground. That's just the way Lisa felt, too!

Lorraine flew past her on Barq.

"Come here, boy!" Lisa said to Pepper, pulling herself to her feet.

"You okay, Lisa?" Max called along the trail.

"Oh, sure. Pepper and I just had a disagreement about which way he was going to go!"

She waited a second to be sure nothing hurt and then rambled across the trail to the waiting Pepper.

"Silly boy," she said, patting his neck, and lifting the reins back over his head. "Silly me, too, I guess, huh?" She lifted her left leg up to the stirrup.

Just then, Max arrived by her side. "Will you be able to ride now?" he asked. "I mean, are you hurt anywhere?"

Lisa paused for just a second before she mounted Pepper. She looked at Max. There was something in the way he asked the question—was he worried about her? No, that wasn't it. Lisa was almost certain he was trying to control a smile—or maybe a laugh.

"I looked pretty silly, didn't I?" she asked, suddenly getting the full impact of what a funny picture she must have made.

"Well, perhaps a little bit undigni-ni-ni—" And then, there was an unmistakable snort of Max's laughter.

Lisa lifted herself up into the saddle and burst into giggles herself. She didn't hurt anyplace. "I guess both getting back on the horse *and* laughing about it are the best cures," she said when she stopped giggling.

"Only when it's funny," he said. And then Lisa realized how fortunate she was!

6

"PSST! WAKE UP!" Lisa whispered, shaking the sleeping Carole from her dreams.

"Whassa matter?" Carole said. She could barely see Lisa in the darkness.

"It's almost dawn!" Lisa said excitedly. "Let's see if there are any deer in the paddock with the horses." Carole was completely awake instantly.

Stevie rubbed her eyes drowsily. "Is it really morning?" she asked.

"Not really," Lisa told her. "But it's time to get up anyway. We're having a Saddle Club meeting down by the paddock."

The three girls crept out of their tent, still wearing their warm nightclothes. They didn't want to take the time to get dressed—not just then, anyway.

They tiptoed on bare feet through the campsite, down the gentle slope to the paddock where the horses spent the night. It was still almost completely dark— the velvet sky was studded with stars. The nearly full moon hung near the horizon and looked as if it were almost resting on a mountaintop. In the east were the first streaks of dawn.

"Oh!" Stevie said, settling herself on a rock near the paddock. "It's beautiful!" She scrunched her knees up to her chest for warmth. Carole sat beside her, Lisa on the other side. Stevie took in a deep breath of the fresh, chilly air. "I can't believe I slept through this yesterday," she said, gazing at the mountains to the east.

The girls sat in a contented silence, listening only to the sounds of the night. The horses, asleep on their feet, were quiet. Here and there, a few crickets chirped. From the edge of the nearby creek, they could hear the call of a bullfrog. The silence was broken by the first whinny from the paddock. In seconds all the horses were awake. By the light of the moon and the stars, the girls watched the horses begin to munch on the sweet grass.

"No deer this morning," Lisa said sadly.

"You never know," Carole said. Suddenly, they all heard a rustling in the forest. Then, so close they could almost touch him, a deer emerged from behind the cover of a hemlock tree. Stevie gasped. Startled, the deer fled, but in a moment, he returned. This time he wasn't alone. The two deer skirted the rock where the girls sat, giving it a wide berth. Then, in unison, they jumped the fence of the paddock, joining the horses at the sweet grass.

The girls were motionless and silent. While they watched in awe, three more deer leaped into the field. The deer eyed the horses with some suspicion, but apparently sensed no harm. Each of the animals munched hungrily, as if it were the most natural thing in the world for horses and deer to breakfast together on a mountainside.

"It's *beautiful!*" Carole whispered to her friends. They nodded. Lisa was about to speak, but just then there was another rustle of leaves nearby. The girls turned to watch the newcomer.

But it wasn't just one newcomer. It was a doe and her baby! The fawn was so little! His head only reached to the top of his mother's legs. His own little legs were long and spindly, with knobby knees—just like a foal's. The doe led her baby to the edge of the field and nibbled the grass under the fence. Her baby nursed while she ate.

The next visitor was smaller—and less welcome. It was a skunk, meandering through the woods with his snout to the ground, sniffing as he went.

"Hey!" Carole exclaimed, pointing to the black-and-white intruder. The three girls pulled their legs up onto the rock to keep out of the skunk's way. The skunk barely seemed to notice them, though. He waddled toward the field and, seeing nothing of interest to his stomach, he waddled away, sniffing everything in his path.

"You know, that one's almost cute," Stevie said to her friends.

"*Almost,*" Lisa agreed. "But don't get him angry!"

"Look!" Carole said, pointing to the eastern horizon. The first of the sun's rays were now over the top of the mountain. A breeze stirred the morning air, bringing the sun's warmth. The horses lifted their heads toward the light. The deer, sensing change, stood alert. The doe fled suddenly, followed by her leggy fawn. And then all the other deer followed, abandoning the sweet grass for the safety of the mountain forest, springing over the fence.

"Did it really happen?" Stevie asked when the deer were gone.

"Yes, it really did," Carole assured her. She stood up and walked toward the paddock fence. She whistled. All the horses looked at her. Cobalt broke from the pack, trotting over for his morning greeting. Lisa and Stevie joined her, and a few of the other horses came over, looking for oats.

"Not yet, guys," Carole said. "Not time for breakfast yet. First we have to—Yipes!"

"What is it?" Stevie asked.

"We've got to get back to camp and put some clothes on before Max and the boys see us in our pajamas!"

In a split second, the girls headed back to their tent. They arrived, puffing and breathless, just an instant before they heard Max's voice call out "Morning time! Everybody up! Time for breakfast! No dawdling today!"

Quickly, Lisa, Stevie, and Carole shed their night-clothes and slipped back into their riding clothes.

"That was the best Saddle Club meeting we ever had!" Lisa said excitedly.

"I wish they could all be like that," Stevie agreed.

"So do I," Carole said. "Gee, remember how beautiful it was when the deer—"

"Stevie!" Max barked. "Your turn to get water for us. Lisa! I need some more kindling! Carole! You're on oats today!"

He almost broke the mood, but not quite. "I remember," Stevie assured Carole. "I'll always remember."

"Yeah, forever," Lisa said. And that was how they all felt.

"I CAN'T BELIEVE it's almost over," Carole said wistfully.

The bright sunshine sparkled through the early-summer leaves in the forest. The day, which had begun in the cool darkness, was now bright and hot, and it was almost time to stop for lunch. Max told the riders to dismount and walk their horses for the last half mile or so, to cool them down.

"Yeah, and to warm *us* up!" Stevie said.

They all laughed about that.

Carole sighed. Horses seemed to her to be a gift, a fabulous, wonderful, magical gift. What she wanted to do most in the world was to take care of horses. That was why she'd agreed to do extra chores for Max at the stable. Her father's salary as a Marine Corps colonel could cover riding lessons and anything else she wanted (as long as she didn't develop Veronica-like tastes). But she worked at the stable because that's what she wanted to do, forever. It's what she'd always wanted to do. Except right now, when she was having fun with the idea of running away with Delilah.

"You know, I think I could build a nice little lean-to near that bluff we passed this morning. Two lean-tos, one for me, one for Delilah. We'd live there, ride every day, and have a great view of the Blue Ridge Mountains. What do you think of that?" Carole asked.

"I think it's time to get you back to civilization," Stevie said matter-of-factly.

"I guess," Carole said. "But it's been wonderful, hasn't it?"

"I could have done without the spill I took yesterday afternoon," Lisa confided. "I'm going to have a bruise in a place I don't want to mention!"

"It's not so bad the *second* time you fall off, is it?" Stevie asked her. "I mean, you knew enough to climb right back onto Pepper, right?"

"*Very* carefully!" Lisa said, and they all giggled. "But I guess it's better than the bee sting Adam got on his arm."

"Those things happen on a camp-out," Carole said. "But—"

"Oooooh! Look!" Stevie said, cutting her off. Carole turned to see a spectacular sight. The little creek that had been running gently near the trail, crossing it several times, suddenly joined another little creek

from high up on the mountain. Together they tumbled
down a dramatic rocky waterfall into a small natural
pond.

"It's *beautiful!*" Lisa said.

Carole stared for a moment, awestruck, then carefully walked Delilah down the incline. Of course, Max
had known this was here. He had picked this spot for
lunch, where the horses could drink and where the
riders could swim!

It took only a few minutes to tie the horses to trees
and to let them have a bit of water and some hay.

"Okay, girls, go change in the woods on the far side
of the pond. The guys will stay on this side. Last one
in is a rotten egg!" Max yelled.

The girls met the challenge. Even Veronica
couldn't wait to jump into the cool mountain water.
Clothes were flung over every branch in the heat of the
race for the water. The girls grabbed their bathing suits
out of their backpacks and slid into them. Stevie found
a path to the pond, and the sweat and grime of two
days of riding quickly disappeared as The Saddle Club
plunged with the other girls into the crystal-clear
pond. Cuts, bumps, bruises, and bug bites were forgot-
ten in the cool water.

"This is *wonderful,*" Lisa said. "Maybe even better
than riding—" Carole shot her a mock dirty look.
"Just joking," she assured Carole. Carole smiled.

When they were completely refreshed, when the
splash fights had subsided (the girls swore they'd won),
and when hunger overcame the riders, they emerged

from the pond to find that their picnic was ready for them.

Exhausted, and totally content, everybody sat down on the soft, mossy ground, and ate.

"Except for that awful spider and the gross bee bite you got, Adam, this has been a fun trip," Veronica said.

Carole looked at her, more than a little surprised. Veronica wasn't one for roughing it. She'd seemed to be having a hard time of it without her family gardeners, cooks, and chauffeurs to ease the way for her.

"Oh, I could just live like this, couldn't you?" Carole asked her, suddenly feeling at one with everybody, even Veronica.

"Live like this?" Veronica asked, in genuine surprise. "Oh, no. I mean, I've had a good time and all, but I don't even want to look at a horse for a week."

"Mean that?" Carole asked. Veronica nodded. "Want me to exercise Cobalt for you this week?"

"If it means that much to you," Veronica said. It irked Carole that Veronica had to turn it into a favor to Carole, but she was eager to take care of Cobalt.

"I'll do it," she said.

Veronica smiled sweetly. Then she stood up and brought out the saddlebags stuffed with candies that her mother had given her in the parking lot.

"I can't drag these home," she explained as she offered them to the riders. "Mother will never forgive me. Eat all you want."

They were wonderful Italian hard candies, sweet and tart all at the same time. And, Carole was certain, as expensive as could be! What a strange girl Veronica was. Just then, Stevie and Lisa caught her eye. The three of them exchanged glances, all as confused by Veronica as ever.

No, Carole told herself. *This day, this trip—they are too wonderful to be ruined by Veronica.* Content once again, she slipped back into the chilly waters of the pond for one last swim; they'd soon be taking their final ride before they had to return to Pine Hollow.

THE WHOLE RIDE back in the van was quiet. Everyone was tired, but Carole knew it was more than that. The trip had been perfect. It was as if all of them wanted to go over every minute of it in their own minds while it was still fresh so they wouldn't forget anything. Then, quiet as the ride had been, everybody began to shriek when they arrived back at Pine Hollow.

The driveway there was filled with cars and station wagons, waiting for the kids. Everybody wanted to tell everything all at once. Mothers, fathers, brothers, and sisters wanted to know all the details, and the riders wanted to share.

Backpacks and bedrolls were unloaded and loaded, switched around, emptied, dumped. Bug bites were displayed.

"You mean you actually camped out in the woods for *two* nights?" Stevie's younger brother, Michael, demanded. He was a scout, and of the opinion that camping was for boys, not girls.

Stevie glared at him. "Yessss," she hissed. But she hugged him anyway. She'd missed him a little. And she'd missed her twin, Alex, and her older brother, Chad. Her mother and father greeted her warmly as well. While she put her things in the back of the station wagon, she was happy to see that the Atwoods were smothering Lisa with welcoming hugs, too.

Carole, she knew, had planned to help Max unload the horses. Her father would come for her later.

Happy, tired, sweaty, dirty, sore, and thrilled, the riders climbed into the waiting cars, ready to go home, but wishing that the camp-out had never ended.

WHEN THE FINAL car door slammed, and the last station wagon pulled out of the drive, Carole, Max, and Red turned to the task of unloading the horses from the trailers.

Carole put Delilah in her stall and then returned for Cobalt. He followed her down the ramp without any difficulty. There was something wonderfully familiar about the clumping of his hooves on the wide wooden boards of the stable's floor. Like the riders, the horses—especially Cobalt—seemed happy to be home. Contentedly, he walked into his stall. But then he turned around right away to look out the window. Carole knew just how he felt.

"Don't worry, boy," she said to him, patting his neck gently. "We'll go back there. One day, you and I will go back to the mountains. We'll climb the hills and canter through the valleys. We'll splash in the ponds and the waterfall. We'll ride together."

And someday they would, she was sure. Until then, at least they could ride in the ring every day this week. It wasn't everything, but it was something.

Carole sighed and then slid the door closed on Cobalt's stall. It was time to go home.

"THERE'S SOMETHING I don't understand," Carole told Max Thursday afternoon while she was saddling Cobalt.

"What's that?" he asked, smoothing the saddle pad for her.

"It's that Veronica always complains that Cobalt is difficult." She lifted the saddle and placed it firmly on the horse's back. Then she slid it into place and reached for the girth.

"You do understand," Max said. "You're just being polite."

"Maybe." Carole shrugged, knowing that was Max's way of saying she was a much better rider than Veronica.

"But I'll tell you this," he continued. "I never approved of Mr. diAngelo buying a stallion for Veronica to ride. A gelding or a mare would be much better for a young rider. A stallion like Cobalt has got an awful lot of spirit. It takes a very skilled rider to handle a stallion. Veronica isn't one; you are."

Carole really didn't know what to say to Max. He rarely complimented his students. Most of them—including Carole—were thrilled with an "okay" or a "that's better" from him. And that was all most of them got.

"I shouldn't complain, though," Max confided. "Cobalt is a Thoroughbred with fine bloodlines. It's an honor to have him in my stable."

Horses, Carole knew, were always evaluated by their bloodlines, meaning who their parents were, and *their* parents. It wasn't the least bit unusual to know a hundred years' worth of breeding history for the better horses, like Cobalt. And, since horses tended to pass on predictable characteristics like speed and temperament to their offspring, it could be extremely important to know that those characteristics were part of the family history carried in the bloodlines.

"I know that running fast and jumping high are in his bloodlines," Carole told Max. "But what constantly amazes me is how smart he is. You know what I got him to do yesterday? I got him to bow! Can you believe it?"

"I was watching from my office," Max said. "I was pretty impressed." There was a sly grin on his face.

"Oh, I know it's silly show-off rodeo stuff," she said. "But it was like he *wanted* to do it. After only about four tries, he just did it."

"Well, today why don't you see if you can teach him something more useful?" Max said.

"I thought we'd work on sideways movements and circles today, and then tomorrow, if it's okay with you, we'll just have a fun ride on the trail."

"And on Saturday?" Max asked.

"On Saturday, Veronica will ride him in class. I won't be here this weekend at all. Dad and I are taking a trip together. He has to go to Camp Lejeune for the Corps and I get to go along." Carole adjusted the stirrups to the right length for her lanky legs.

"You have family down there in North Carolina, don't you?"

"Yes, I'm staying at Aunt Elaine's. She's my mother's sister. We aren't coming back until Tuesday. Dad got special permission for me to miss school."

"He didn't ask me if you could miss riding school," Max said.

For a second, Carole was afraid he was serious, but when she looked at his suntanned face and saw the sparkle in his sky-blue eyes, she knew it was a joke.

"Have a good time," Max said. "But don't fall for any of those Nowth Cahalaina howses, yuh heah?!" he teased in a southern accent.

"No way!" Carole told him, laughing. "There's only one horse for me and he's right here!"

Carole led Cobalt out of his stall and over to the entrance to the ring. She slipped her left foot into the stirrup and lifted herself up. As she settled into the saddle, she saw a look of concern cross Max's face. But when she looked again, it was gone. Clucking softly to Cobalt, she brought him out into the ring, remembering to touch the stable's "good-luck horseshoe" nailed on the wall by the mounting block.

That horseshoe was one of Pine Hollow's oldest traditions. Every rider touched it before beginning a ride. As long as anybody could remember, nobody had ever been seriously hurt riding at Pine Hollow. Carole was pretty sure that the *real* reason for that safety record was because Max (and Maxes I and II) had always been very fussy about the quality of riding at Pine Hollow, but it didn't stop her from touching the horseshoe every time she mounted. It also didn't stop her from riding very carefully.

"COME ON, BOY," Carole urged Cobalt. "Over to the left. You can do it."

She knew perfectly well that Cobalt didn't understand the words, but hearing her voice seemed to give him confidence. She was working with him on lateral, or sideways, moves. Usually riders practiced moving a horse forward, and sometimes backward, but for the experienced rider, sideways could be just as important. It was often essential for shows, demonstrating the rider's ability to control the horse and the horse's ability to respond to commands.

Today Carole wanted to teach Cobalt to turn on the forehand—and she wanted to learn it herself.

Holding the reins short enough so that she knew for sure when she was putting pressure on Cobalt's mouth, she moved her right leg back a very little bit and pressed on Cobalt's side. First, he stepped forward. She drew the reins inward to stop his forward movement and held them there. Then, she pressed again with her right leg.

It worked! Cobalt's right rear leg stepped to the left, his left leg following, while his front legs remained stable, shifting only to pivot. Carole did this several more times and, before she knew it, the horse had turned completely around a circle, with his front legs at the center of it.

"Good boy!" she said, patting his neck firmly. "Good boy! I knew you could do it! Let's try it again, okay?"

Cobalt stretched his neck. Carole could have sworn he was nodding to her, but she knew better. After all, how many times had Max told her horses couldn't understand English? A lot of them learned to respond to words like "trot" and "canter" if they heard them during a class and there were other horses doing those paces already. Some days it seemed to Carole that they could tell time, too, the way they started heading for their stalls when an hour-long class was *almost* over. But those things were really the result of training, not an understanding of language or clocks. It was the same as when she got fidgety in her math class after about thirty-eight minutes—or sometimes only three minutes!

Cobalt, however, seemed to understand more. Maybe it was more than Carole's words and tone of voice. Part of it, she was sure, was how well she could feel his movements under her with her legs and with her seat. It was logical that he was as sensitive to her on top of him.

Standing still once again, she tried a turn on the forehand to the right. Cobalt executed it perfectly, as if he'd been doing it all his life.

How on earth, she wondered, could Veronica own this wonderful animal and not want to spend every waking minute with him?

"I know you're going to miss me, boy," she said, leaning forward in her saddle, stroking the horse's glistening black coat. "But I won't be gone long. I'll be back in a couple of days. We'll ride together again soon—just you and me, Cobalt."

Carole nudged Cobalt with her heels and he began a regal walk around the ring. As they passed Max's office window, it suddenly flew open. Max stuck his head out.

"Looks like you and Cobalt had a pretty good session. But how many times do I have to tell you that horses don't understand English?" he said, only half-joking.

"Don't worry, Max," she shot back. "It's not English. I'm teaching him Swahili!"

Max shook his head, then pulled it back in and shut the window firmly. Carole signaled Cobalt to pick up the pace. Soon they were cantering around the ring, smooth as glass, fast as the wind.

CAROLE'S FOUR-DAY visit with Aunt Elaine was every bit as nice as she'd thought it was going to be. While Colonel Hanson worked, Carole and her aunt chatted, gossiped, and giggled together while taking care of Elaine's three young boys. She and Aunt Elaine even spent one morning horseback riding along the beach. It was fun, but it wasn't the same as riding Cobalt. It felt wonderfully wicked to be excused from school for two days without even being sick, but when it came time to go home, Carole was ready. Saying good-bye to her aunt's family was hard, though. It seemed as if she couldn't give or get enough hugs until she thought about how much she wanted to see Cobalt again.

"So you enjoyed it, did you?" her father asked as they drove back home from the airport.

"I had a great time with Aunt Elaine," Carole said. "She's just fun to be with. So are her kids."

"I know you miss your mother," Colonel Hanson began. "I miss her, too. I try to fill in, but there are some things . . ."

The time since her mother's death the previous fall had been hard on both of them. Carole knew that her father had worried a lot about trying to be both mother and father to her, but as far as she was concerned, he was her father and that was great.

"Don't worry about that, Daddy. I had fun with Aunt Elaine, even though sometimes she reminded me of Mom. She does look like her, doesn't she? But as far as parents go, you're enough for me—at least until you meet some wonderful woman and decide to get married again," she added with a sly grin.

"Now, don't you start in," her father said.

"Oh, Aunt Elaine gave you a hard time, huh? She told me she thought you should get married again. Is that why she kept having all her 'friends' at the house when you were there?"

"I think so. And I had thought I'd get some relief from that when we got away from home."

Carole had to laugh. Almost every one of their friends seemed to know a single woman who would be "just perfect" for Carole's father. "You know what Marjorie Jennings—you know, the major's daughter—told me? She said that the ladies in the bridge league at the Officers' Club at Quantico call you 'Colonel Handsome.' Of course, they're right. You're the handsomest man I know. And you look so *dashing* in your uniform—especially the dress blues with the red stripe!" she teased her father.

He laughed. "And don't you think for a minute that Mrs. Jennings hasn't invited her unmarried sister down for a visit. Every time I see the woman, she tells me how wonderful her sister is and what a *marvelous* mother she'd make. See, Carole, it isn't just *me* they're after. The woman wants to be a mother to *you*. Are you ready for that?"

"Not from any sister of Mrs. Jennings's!" Carole said, laughing. "But Dad, seriously, wouldn't you like to get married again?"

"Well, hon, I'll tell you. I loved your mom. She was one in a million—no, make that two million. There just isn't anybody to replace her."

Carole was quiet for a moment. Her father was often very lonely without her mother. She knew that one day he would probably find another woman to share his life with. Until he was ready, or until the right woman came along, nothing she could say would make it happen.

"Especially Mrs. Jennings's sister," Carole said.

"And *especially* if she looks like Mrs. Jennings!"

"A fine thing for you to say, Colonel Handsome!" Carole chided him. They laughed together. Carole felt then, as she had felt many times since her mother's death, that losing her mother was the most awful thing

that could have happened to her. But she still had her
father, and a pretty terrific one at that. One in two
million.

A HALF HOUR later, Carole's suitcase was unpacked
and she was beginning to feel as if she were actually
back home again. That made it time to call Stevie and
Lisa. Maybe they could all get together at the Tastee
Delight ice cream parlor—TD's, as the girls called
their favorite meeting place. But just as she reached for
the phone, it rang.

"Hello?"

"Oh, Carole, you're back!" Stevie said.

"Right on time," Carole said cheerfully. "I was just
about to call you. I had a wonderful time in North
Carolina. I can't wait to tell you and Lisa all about it.
Saddle Club meeting tomorrow right after school? We
can meet at TD's for ice cream—"

"Carole, stop!" Stevie said. "You've got to get over
here."

"You missed me that badly, huh?" Carole teased.
But when there was a silence, Carole began to get the
awful feeling that something was wrong. Really wrong.
"Where are you? What's the matter?"

"I'm at Pine Hollow. It's Cobalt—I mean, just get
over here, will you?"

"*What?*" she said, but Stevie had already hung up
the phone.

In a matter of minutes, Carole and her father were back in their car, this time headed for Pine Hollow. Carole was so worried she couldn't speak. Her father just squeezed her hand and said, "It's going to be all right, hon. You'll see."

As they neared the stable, Carole could hear the terrible whine of a siren. An ambulance pulled out of the driveway and turned toward the hospital, lights flashing, siren wailing. The diAngelos' Mercedes was parked carelessly in the lot, its doors left open.

But the only things Carole really saw were the veterinarian's pickup truck and the county vet's wagon. That was when Carole knew the worst. Two veterinarians always had to sign a certificate before a horse could be destroyed.

"*Cobalt!*" she screamed, jumping from the car almost before it stopped.

Lisa and Stevie came running out of the stable. Lisa reached Carole first and put her arm around her. Stevie had tears streaming down her face.

"It's too late, Carole," she said. "He was too badly hurt! They had to do it. He would never heal. It was the long bone in his foreleg—it was shattered. He just lay there. And then it was over."

"And then the ambulance came for Veronica," Lisa continued. "She's going to be okay. I guess she broke her arm. She was lucky. Luckier than Cobalt." Lisa gasped at her own words, trying to hold back tears.

Carole stared blankly at the stable, wanting to go in, wanting to go away. She remembered feeling like that once before. She stood still, unable to move, until her father came up to her and put his strong arms around her shoulders.

"Come on home, hon," he said. "There's nothing we can do here."

"*Cobalt!*" she sobbed.

Slowly, she turned, letting her father take her home.

"WE'VE GOT TO help Carole," Lisa said. "She was like a zombie at school today." She and Stevie were walking toward Carole's house the day after the accident that had cost Cobalt his life.

"I think Carole's going to have to get over this herself," Stevie warned Lisa. She wanted to comfort Carole, but she knew that sympathy and comfort could only go so far.

"Carole showed me how important it was to get back on the horse when I fell off. This is different, I know, but in some ways it's the same. We can't let her feel too sorry for herself."

"I don't think she's feeling sorry for herself. If I know Carole, she's feeling sorry for Cobalt."

"Well, just wait until we tell her what happened when we saw Veronica at the hospital, then," Lisa said.

"That may just make her feel sorrier for Cobalt," Stevie said, shaking her head. She just couldn't understand the whole diAngelo family.

Carole was in her room when her friends arrived. She'd gone to school that morning, but she didn't think she'd heard anyone or learned a single thing. As soon as she got home, she retreated to her bedroom. She was lying on her bed, staring at the ceiling, when Stevie and Lisa knocked.

"Your dad said it was okay for us to come up," Stevie said, poking her head in the room.

Carole sighed deeply. She knew her friends had come to make her feel better. She also knew that they felt badly about Cobalt's accident and maybe they needed somebody to make them feel better, too. She only wished she could have made Cobalt better. But, of course, she couldn't.

"Sure, come on in," Carole told the girls. They came in and sat on her bed with her. Stevie handed her a soda. Carole took a sip and nodded thanks. "I guess you'd better tell me exactly what happened. I really didn't want to know yesterday, but I think I'm ready now."

"It was Veronica's fault," Lisa began, confirming Carole's suspicions. "It was just exactly what Max had been telling her not to do on the camp-out. We were all there—it was a jumping class on the cross-country course. I was watching with Max. Stevie had just gone over the jump on Comanche. Veronica came barreling down the hill at a gallop and expected Cobalt to jump a high fence, landing on a downhill slope."

"He had such a big heart, you know, Carole. He just always wanted to please his rider—even when he knew it was wrong. He didn't slow down one bit. He just jumped," Stevie said.

"It was beautiful in a way," Lisa continued. "There's no horse in that stable that jumps as smoothly as Cobalt—jumped, I mean—but he didn't land right."

"I saw it then, too," Stevie said. "It was like he was flying, until his front legs landed. There was just too much of him, coming too fast. His forelegs hit the ground straight and then the right one buckled, but not at the knee. He began to stumble."

"Veronica flew off over his head. She landed five feet in front of him. She broke her arm when she landed. Cobalt broke his leg. Everybody could see it was broken. . . ."

Stevie and Lisa went on, describing the horrible scene that Carole had been reliving in her mind for the past twenty-four hours: Veronica screaming her head off; Cobalt lying quietly, bearing his pain in silence.

Sometimes when horses broke bones, they could be set, like people's bones, and they could heal and be

as good as new. With the horse's cannon bone,
though, it was almost impossible to keep the horse's
weight off the break long enough for it to heal. A million-dollar racehorse might be suspended in a body
sling long enough for the bone to knit, but even then,
with a broken cannon bone, he'd probably never race
again. Although Cobalt was a fine horse with good
bloodlines, he was no million-dollar horse, and that
kind of treatment was too expensive and not reliable
enough. And, even if the bone could have healed,
he'd never have been as good as new, and he'd have
been in pain all his life.

"If only they could have tried something to save
him," Lisa said.

"No," Carole told her. "They did the right thing.
Cobalt's life was over. He was born to run with the
wind, not limp."

Stevie got the feeling it was time to change the
subject a little. "Say, we just saw Veronica. We visited
her at St. Claire's. She's got a private room and there
are nurses running all over the place."

"Was she hurt that badly? I thought it was just a
broken arm."

"It was, but you know her parents," Lisa said. Carole nodded. They all knew her parents. They were the
richest people in town and liked to show it off. "You'd
think she'd had open-heart surgery from all the attention she was demanding—and the flowers!"

"It looked like a funeral!" Stevie said.

"It was," Carole told her friends. Stevie and Lisa exchanged looks.

"Well, Veronica was all full of talk about how Max wasn't a very good teacher and this would never have happened if it hadn't been for him."

"That's outrageous!" Carole said. "We all heard Max tell her a hundred times she was jumping the wrong way. How can she—"

"That's not even really the worst of it," Stevie said, full of indignation. "Her father was prancing around the room telling her not to worry—that they were going to get plenty of insurance money for Cobalt and she'd have another horse as soon as her arm healed. Can you believe trying to replace Cobalt?"

Carole shook her head. "That sounds like the di-Angelos," she said. "They think they can solve every problem with money."

"Oh, he'll have a new horse for Veronica soon, that's for sure," Lisa said.

"Well, he won't be able to make her ride it," Carole said.

"She'll ride it for sure," Stevie said. "The trick will be to make her ride it *right.*"

"What makes you think she'll ever get on a horse again?" Carole asked.

Stevie almost laughed. "Of course she will! She said she would and we both believed her. She may not be horse crazy the way we are, but she likes riding and she knows accidents happen. She knows you have to get back on—the same way you do."

"Not me," Carole said.

Stevie was startled. Had she heard Carole right? "What?" she asked.

"I said not me. I'm done riding. For good."

Lisa and Stevie both stared at her. Was it possible? Carole was the best. Her life was riding. She was the one who was going to own a stable, was going to teach, was going to train and breed horses. Horses were everything to her. It couldn't be true, Stevie was sure.

"Oh, that's the way you feel now, I know, but you won't feel that way always. You'll start riding again. You love it too much."

"I don't expect you two to understand," Carole said. "But Cobalt was more than just a horse to me. There could never be another horse like that. With him gone, there's no point in riding. Anyway, this is kind of hard to explain, but when I was outside the stable yesterday, knowing that he was gone and he wasn't coming back, it reminded me of the day my mother died. I don't ever want to feel that way again. So I'm quitting."

"Carole!" Lisa said, her voice filled with worry.

"Lisa, I think we should get to the bus stop now," Stevie said, cutting her off.

Lisa was about to remind Stevie that her mother was picking them up at Carole's in an hour when she saw the look on Stevie's face and clammed up.

"We do?"

"Yeah, sure," she agreed. "Will you be okay, Carole? I'll see you in school tomorrow."

Carole nodded.

Lisa and Stevie backed out of her room and quickly went downstairs. Colonel Hanson was in the kitchen making dinner.

"It's bad, isn't it?" he asked the girls.

"Yeah," Stevie said. "She says she doesn't want to ride again."

"Well, if she wants to give it up, that's her choice," the colonel said.

"But it's not a choice!" Lisa protested. "It's some kind of phony escape. Horses are too important to her."

"Well, certainly *one* horse was," Stevie said.

"We'll just have to see what happens," Carole's father said. Stevie and Lisa reluctantly agreed with that.

"I DON'T UNDERSTAND Carole," Lisa said as she and Stevie waited around the corner from Carole's house for Mrs. Atwood to pick them up.

"I'm not sure I do, either. But it looks like a bad case of horse shyness, like after an accident. This time, she can't just climb back up on the horse—because the horse isn't there. I have the feeling that nothing we say or do will help. She'll have to come around on her own. Look, are we horse crazy, or what?" Stevie asked.

"We're horse crazy," Lisa agreed.

"So, our only choice is to keep riding and try to help Carole come around. After all, she's horse crazy, too, but right now, she's more crazy than she is horse. You'll be at class on Saturday, won't you?"

"Of course," Lisa told her.

"So, we'll ride and then, afterward, we have some work to do."

"We do?"

"Yeah, remember how we planned to do research on Max the First?"

"Oh, yeah, we want to find out if he really was in the Russian Revolution."

"I think we know he wasn't there, but the question is: Where was he? You said we should start in the library."

"Right! We can look at the back issues of *The Willow Creek Gazette*. That'll be fun." Lisa knew that Stevie was right. At least the two of them would continue riding and having fun together. But she wondered how long The Saddle Club would survive with just two members

11

"YOU'RE REALLY LEARNING fast, Lisa!" Stevie complimented her after class on Saturday. "Your seat is much
firmer, your contact is better. I mean, you're riding!"

"It seems like months ago that I didn't know anything about horses—except for which was the front
end and which wasn't. But, actually, it's only weeks,
right?"

"If you keep on learning at the rate you're going
now, it'll seem like years when it's only weeks. And
then, when school's out and summer starts, we'll be
able to ride almost every day. You'll be a champion by
August."

"You mean I'll be as good as you?" Lisa teased.

Stevie, who was very proud of her own hard-earned
riding skills, glanced sideways at Lisa. When she saw

the sly grin on the older girl's face, she knew Lisa was joking.

"Oh, that'll happen about the same day Max sprouts wings!"

"I noticed some feathers on his back today," Lisa joked.

Together, the two girls walked back into town. Each had come to riding class armed with notebook, pencil, and library card.

The sun was shining brightly off the sidewalk. It was a hot Saturday, promising an even hotter summer to come. It was a day to sit by a pool—or better yet, *in* a pool—not one to be at the library. But the unspoken agreement between Lisa and Stevie was that as long as they worked hard together on a Saddle Club project (like finding out who the *real* Max the First was), then they might not have to think so much about the death of Cobalt or how much they missed Carole at class.

"Excuse me," Lisa said politely to the woman at the information desk. "We want to do some research on history—"

"Section nine hundred, the shelves to your left," the woman said briskly.

"Specifically, American—"

"Section nine hundred seventy, the first eight shelves." The librarian rattled off the information without looking up.

"Well, really, Virginia—" Lisa continued.

"Section nine hundred seventy-three, shelves five and six."

"Actually, Willow Creek, early this century."

"Section—Willow Creek?" For the first time, the librarian looked at Lisa and Stevie. "I don't think anybody's ever actually written a book about Willow Creek."

Suddenly, the woman was interested. She took Stevie and Lisa to the card file, but it was clear that there wasn't a book.

"How about old newspapers?" Lisa asked. Stevie was very glad she had Lisa the A-student on this trip.

"Ah, yes!" the librarian exclaimed. "At the insistence of the editor of *The Willow Creek Gazette*, we have five complete sets of every newspaper ever issued in this town. Be my guest, but be careful. Some of this stuff is very old and the paper is delicate."

She led Stevie and Lisa into a small room off the main reading room. She turned on the light and showed them the big old books containing over a hundred years of news.

"If you consider Mrs. Rappaport's garden party news," Stevie said a few minutes later, glancing through a musty old volume.

Lisa took one of the volumes off the shelf. "The trouble is that not only do we not know what we're looking for, we don't even know *when* we're looking for. I'll start in 1920. You work through Mrs. Rappaport's social season of 1905. It's probably somewhere between the two. We'll work toward each other."

Stevie nodded, pulling her notebook over to where she could reach it in case something interesting showed up. Two hours later, she knew an awful lot about the sewer system the town had installed and a great deal about the Rappaports' guest lists, but she didn't know anything at all about Maxmillian Regnery the First.

"I keep seeing the same advertisement for riding lessons," Lisa said. "The ad just refers to The Stable at Pine Hollow, but I guess that's the same one. There's no address and no name. The one thing I can say is that riding lessons were a lot cheaper then than they are now!"

Stevie peered over her shoulder at the ad. It showed an old-fashioned picture of a lady—"Probably Mrs. Rappaport," Stevie said—riding sidesaddle on a fine horse. It was fun to see, but it really didn't help them at all.

"There aren't any stable ads in the 1905 papers. It took me a while to figure out that in 1905, almost everybody owned horses since that was the way most people got around. They had their own stables, same as we have our own garages. There are ads for black-smiths, but that's as close as we get here."

"I'm still sure this is the thing to do if we want to find out about Max," Lisa said.

"Oh, I agree," Stevie told her. "But I don't think we've hit it yet. And that's all the musty old news-papers I want to read today."

"Me too," Lisa said, slipping the big volume back onto the shelf. Together, they finished tidying up, turned out the light in the little room, and left the library, thanking the surprised librarian on their way out.

"We'll be back!" Lisa promised.

"You're welcome anytime!" the woman said cheerfully. Lisa had the distinct impression that the librarian would call the editor of the *Gazette* to tell him that somebody was actually reading the back issues. It would make his day. But so far, it hadn't done anything for theirs.

"You know, that's not the only source we have," Lisa said after a moment.

"Sure, we can check with the crystal ball lady at the fair when she comes to town in August," Stevie said.

"Crystal balls are supposed to tell the future, not the past," Lisa said, giggling. "No, what I mean is that, for one thing, we could try official records at town hall and—" she paused, "*and* we can try pumping Mrs. Reg. After all, the man was her father-in-law. She might have some juicy tidbits for us."

"Hey, great idea," Stevie said. "I never thought of that. Why don't we get to the stable early on Tuesday before class and see if she'll give us some hints?"

"It's a date," Lisa agreed.

"WHAT ARE YOU two doing here?" Mrs. Reg asked when Stevie and Lisa walked into the tack room Tuesday afternoon.

Lisa felt trapped and was glad when Stevie answered the question. "Oh, we just thought we'd do some saddle-soaping before class," she said airily.

Mrs. Reg looked at her suspiciously. Lisa knew they were on thin ice. Although they'd both worked hard at the stable (all of Max's students worked hard at the stable; Max insisted that taking care of horses was an important part of riding them), it was Carole who usually wanted to clean the tack. Lisa was sure Mrs. Reg would see right through them.

The woman stood up and went to the shelf where the cleaning gear was kept. "Here you go, girls," she said, handing each of them a tin of saddle soap, sponges, and cloths. "The bridles over on that wall need cleaning today." Her voice softened. "I'm glad to see you here. I miss Carole. She's the best soaper we ever had."

"She's the best at a lot of stuff," Lisa said.

"Yeah, we miss her, too. That's why we wanted to help you today," Stevie agreed.

The girls took their gear and headed for the bridles. There sure were a lot of them. It looked like an endless job—almost as endless as Mrs. Rappaport's garden parties!

"Say, Mrs. Reg," Stevie began casually while she worked the dirt out of a throatlatch.

"Hmm?" Mrs. Reg responded.

"How about that guy, Maxmillian the First, was he something?"

"Who?" asked Mrs. Reg.

"You know, Max's grandfather—the founder of this place? He was your father-in-law, right?"

"Oh, sure," Mrs. Reg said.

Lisa could see that Stevie was trying to lay a trap for Mrs. Reg. She wanted to get her talking about the old man without her really noticing it. Lisa held her breath, hoping.

"I mean, like when he opened the stable—" Stevie paused. Lisa hoped Mrs. Reg would pick up the idea and start talking.

"Hmmm," was all the older woman said.

"It was a long time ago, right?" Stevie prompted.

"Uh, yes," Mrs. Reg told them. She was shuffling through papers on her desk. "I suppose it seems that way, if you're twelve years old."

That was a rebuff if Lisa had ever heard one!

"But were you around then?" Stevie asked.

"I'm not sure," Mrs. Reg said.

This conversation was definitely not going the way the girls wanted it to go.

"Well, what was he like?" Stevie asked. Lisa could tell she'd decided to be more direct. Being indirect was getting them exactly nowhere.

"Who?" Mrs. Reg asked. Being direct was getting them nowhere, too.

"Your father-in-law," Stevie persisted.

"Oh, he was a fine rider," Mrs. Reg told the girls.

"Where did he learn to ride?" Stevie asked.

"Everybody rode in those days," Mrs. Reg said.

And that was all they could get out of her. When Lisa and Stevie looked up from their bridles, they could see that Mrs. Reg's eyes were sparkling with mischief. They realized that they were not the first Pine Hollow students to try to pump her about the stable's founder—nor were they the only ones who weren't going to get anything from her.

"It's a conspiracy!" Stevie hissed to Lisa. "They won't tell us *anything*. The old man was probably a bank robber—or a horse thief! We'll get to the bottom of this!"

Lisa was becoming as convinced as Stevie that the mystery was a cover-up, and she was as determined as Stevie to uncover it. The problem was that right then their curiosity had only earned them the right to clean bridles. They were stuck.

"Have you girls talked to Carole?" Mrs. Reg asked, breaking the silence.

"Yeah, we went to visit her on Saturday. She's going to quit riding, you know?" Lisa said.

"So my son told me," Mrs. Reg said. "She really loved that horse, didn't she?"

Stevie nodded. "He was a beauty," she said, thinking of how magnificent Cobalt had been. She could see him soaring over jumps with Carole in the saddle. She felt a lump in her throat. She set her jaw firmly. She didn't want to cry. She began rubbing the bridle harder to keep her mind off Cobalt.

"There'll never be another horse like that for Carole," Lisa told Mrs. Reg. "And if she can't have a horse like that, she doesn't want any horse at all. I think I can understand that." Lisa thought she *could* understand the perfect relationship Carole and Cobalt had enjoyed. She hated to think about it, but she knew it must really hurt to lose someone you loved so much.

"Nonsense!" Mrs. Reg said firmly, startling both of the girls.

"She's serious!" Stevie said, defending her friend.

"Sure she is, but she's also wrong," Mrs. Reg told them. "And she'll realize it one of these days."

"Oh, no!" Lisa said. "She's made up her mind."

"You know, if I could tell you how many fine riders decide at one time or another that they're never going to ride again—well, it would be a long list. But I'll say this: Carole has got horses in her blood. She'll be back. I don't know when, but she'll be back. Count on it."

"You really think so?" Stevie asked.

"Of course I do," Mrs. Reg said. "But I hate to see her waste so much time right now. Say, I've got an idea—"

And when she told them, Stevie and Lisa had to agree with her that it might just work. At least, they'd give it a try.

12

"HI, CAROLE, IT'S me," Stevie said into the phone on Wednesday night. "How've you been?" Stevie and Carole went to different schools. Usually they saw each other at riding class. Now that Carole wasn't going to classes, they weren't seeing each other at all.

"I'm okay," Carole said dully. Stevie thought she sounded anything but okay.

"We missed you at class this week," Stevie told her. "They were good classes, too. Max had us all working on paces and strides. Lisa's doing really well. I think she may be able to talk him into letting her start jumping classes in the fall. He said he'd never seen such a natural rider—since you, I mean."

"Lisa can have the honors now," Carole said.

Stevie was disappointed. She'd wanted to goad Carole into returning to Pine Hollow, but it obviously wasn't going to work. She decided to try Mrs. Reg's suggestion.

"Mrs. Reg said she was going to call you."

"I hope she doesn't want to try to convince me to come back," Carole said.

"Oh, no. She said she understands that. But she told me you'd promised to help her in the tack room. It was something about the trip—" Stevie paused, hoping Carole herself would remember.

"All those extra bits and stirrup leathers!" Carole said. "We just bunched them up and put them in bags when we left on the MTO. I promised her I'd sort them out and put them away when we got back—but can't she do that herself?"

Stevie knew she had to be very careful now. Of course Mrs. Reg could do it herself, but Carole wasn't to know that. "I'm sure she can. Don't worry about it. She'll do it when the pain goes away."

"Pain?" Carole asked. Her voice was filled with concern.

"She said her arthritis was hurting her. All this humidity, you know? She'll get better when it cools down." *Perfect,* Stevie told herself. *You're doing it perfectly.* After all, it wouldn't cool down for months!

"Oh," Carole said. Stevie was quiet for a moment. She just wanted her little bit of information to sink in. What Mrs. Reg knew about Carole was that, above all, she was a kind person. When Carole made a promise, she kept it. When somebody needed her help, she got it.

And when Carole needed help, her friends gave it to her—even if she didn't think she wanted it!

CAROLE FELT VERY awkward when she arrived at Pine Hollow on Saturday. For one thing, she was wearing overalls and a loose shirt and sneakers. She usually wore riding clothes. But she'd always been there before to ride. This time she was only coming to sort out tack. She didn't need to wear riding breeches and boots to sort out tack. In fact, she didn't need to wear breeches and boots ever again. She wasn't going to ride anymore.

She'd waited until the last of her classmates had left after Saturday's lesson. Max was busy with the adults who took a jumping class after the girls' class. Mrs. Reg was, as usual, in her office off the tack room. Carole would go to her—in a few minutes.

She let herself in the side door of the stable. It had been almost two weeks since Cobalt's death—but Carole felt as though she'd been away for months. As soon as she stepped inside, memories came flooding back to her. The smell of hay and horses was sharp and welcoming— but not to her, she told herself. She breathed deeply and waited for her eyes to adjust to the muted light.

Patch stuck his head out over the top of his stall door. Carole automatically reached for his soft nose, rubbing it gently. He nuzzled her neck, but she hadn't brought any tidbits for him. She patted him once again. Next door, Pepper's head popped out of his stall.

It was just like Pepper to want to get in on the patting, Carole laughed to herself. She scratched his forehead and patted his big strong neck.

Pepper was a big horse, almost as big as Cobalt, but he didn't have Cobalt's brilliant, shiny black coat and he didn't have the smooth trot and the wonderful rolling canter that Cobalt had had. He didn't have—Carole stopped these thoughts. They wouldn't bring Cobalt back. Nothing would bring him back. Cobalt's stall was the one just beyond Pepper's. Carole didn't want to see it. Quickly, Carole turned and retreated to the tack room.

"Hi, Mrs. Reg," she said. "I just remembered I promised you I'd straighten out the stuff we took on the MTO. Here I am."

"Oh, hi, Carole. That bag's in the corner. I haven't even opened it. Thanks for coming by."

Carole got the sack and dumped out its contents. She had to laugh at what she saw. Every time somebody had asked her about extra stirrup leathers, she'd put two in the bag. There were dozens there! And they hadn't needed any of them. She began sorting them out, as well as the stirrups, bits, and other miscellaneous items that had been stuffed in—none of which they'd needed. She knew, though, that if she hadn't brought them, stirrup leathers would have been snapping left and right.

"Be careful where you toss it over there," Mrs. Reg said after a moment.

"Why's that?" Carole asked.

"Eclipse just had a litter of kittens last week and they're bedded down in the box in the corner," Mrs. Reg explained.

"Can I look?" Carole asked.

"Sure, just be careful. They're starting to scramble and trying to get out of the box. Every time we have a litter I'm so afraid that the little ones will get hurt, you know?"

"I'll be careful," Carole promised. Quietly, cautiously, she peeked into the box. There, sleeping contentedly, were six little furry kittens. They were so tangled up with one another as they slept that it was impossible to tell where one began and the other one ended. Eclipse, their mother, was awake, watching them proudly. "Oh, Mrs. Reg, they're the cutest ever! Aren't they wonderful?"

"As long as they're good mousers, they're wonderful," Mrs. Reg said, always practical.

Pine Hollow, like all stables, had occasional problems with mice who liked oats almost as much as the horses did. For centuries, horse people had known that the best exterminator in a barn was a hungry cat. Pine Hollow usually had four or five cats, and every once in a while, that meant four or five kittens as well. This time, there were six! "What have you named them?" Carole asked.

At Pine Hollow, the tradition was to name the cats after the most distinguished horses in history. Eclipse, for example, was named after a famous Thoroughbred racehorse from the eighteenth century. The main drawback of this system of naming cats was that the most famous horses were stallions. With a name like Copperbottom, who was a famous Quarter Horse, it didn't matter. But the last litter of kittens had been born to Sir Archie!

"Oh, I haven't decided," Mrs. Reg said. "I think it's about time to use some of the Standardbreds. How about Messenger, Hambletonian, Dutchman, Yankee, Dan Patch?"

"Yes," Carole agreed. "Those are good names. The little black-and-white one has to be Dan Patch—or are those really two kittens all tangled up?" Carole was trying to figure that out when the question was answered for her. Half of the "black-and-white one" woke up. He was completely black and his eyes were barely open. He was so small, he could have sat on the palm of her hand. The kitten stretched and began walking across his brothers and sisters, heading for the side of the box. He stood on his hind feet, his forelegs straddling the rim. He tried to push himself up and over, struggling mightily. He scratched at the side of the box with his hind legs, trying to get a grasp on it to push himself up—and out.

"This black one's trying to get out," Carole said, gently lowering him back toward his sleeping littermates.

"That one's been trying to get out practically since the day he was born. He's smarter than the rest, tougher, stronger. He always feeds first, and he was the first to walk. That one's a handful of trouble, but he's a winner. You want to name him?" Mrs. Reg asked.

Carole watched the kitten a moment. His blue, blue eyes gleamed with curiosity about the world. Then the sun caught his black coat and it shone brightly, almost a blue-black. Carole had seen a coat like that before. She'd known an animal with a heart like that before. She knew what name that little kitten had earned. But she couldn't say it.

"Maybe," she told Mrs. Reg. "I'll think about it."

Carole turned to the mixed-up pile of leathers and bits she had to sort.

"You know, I was thinking the other day about a horse I once rode," Mrs. Reg said.

Mrs. Reg had ridden horses all her life until her arthritis made it impossible. She'd known horses and horse people. She had wonderful stories to tell and Carole always enjoyed listening to them. It made her work with the tack pass quickly. Carole tugged at the long leather straps, trying to untangle them, and listened with pleasure.

"She was a fine horse, that one. Her name was Lady Day. She was a Saddlebred with wonderful showy gaits, lifting her legs up high with every step, moving smooth as glass. She belonged to the real estate man in town. He used to love to take people to see property in a buggy, pulled by Lady Day. He sold a lot of houses that way, I'll tell you. But when he didn't have customers, she just stayed with us. Max would let her out in the paddock for exercise, but that wasn't enough for her. That one liked to perform. She needed an audience, riding her or watching her.

"So, I took to riding her—with Mr. Marsh's permission, of course. She was as much fun to ride as any horse I've known. She would prance across the fields, pretty and proud as could be. I always sat tall on her back, feeling as proud as she did. And, as you can imagine, when spring rolled around and Mr. Marsh's business got busier and he was using her every day, well, I missed her a lot. She was a winter horse for me, see, because he wouldn't take his customers out in the cold. We were sort of foul-weather friends."

Mrs. Reg stopped talking and Carole waited for her to go on. When she didn't, Carole urged her. "What happened to her?"

"Oh, Mr. Marsh sold her one day—said she'd stumbled pulling his buggy and he couldn't have an animal that wasn't surefooted taking his customers around."

"Was that true?"

"No, I don't think so. I think his business wasn't going so well then and he needed the money."

"But didn't you feel awful when Lady Day was gone?" Carole asked.

"Me? No, not really. But what a horse she was!"

"I never heard you talk about her before. Was she your favorite horse ever?" Carole asked.

"Favorite?" Mrs. Reg said, as if she were considering what the word meant. "I don't think so, though she made me want to own a Saddlebred myself. I nagged Max until he bought one. That one was named Jefferson. Sweetest horse, I'll tell you. Now, he used to wait for me every morning. Old Max would tell you I was crazy, but I swear that horse smiled when he saw me. When I curried him, he never budged. He even stood still for the blacksmith. You gave him a signal to do something, he did it right away. I don't think I ever touched the creature with a riding crop."

"Oh, he must have been a *dream* to ride," Carole said breathlessly.

"Not really," Mrs. Reg told her. "He spent so much time being nice that he had almost no spirit of his own. But that was nothing like old Foxfire."

"Who was Foxfire?" Carole asked.

"Foxfire was a mare we had. She was a fine horse, good to ride, gentle with the youngsters, nice jumper, too. And then we bred her. We wanted to see if we could have that nice temperament carry over another generation."

"Did it?"

"Hard to tell," Mrs. Reg said. "See, as soon as her foal was born—it was a pretty bay colt with a white star on his forehead—Foxfire completely changed personalities. She became so protective of her colt that she wouldn't let anybody near him, or her, for that matter."

"What did you do?" Carole asked.

"We sold them. We sold them both together. Some man from downstate said he was sure he could retrain the mare. Took them away in a van one day and we never heard another word from him."

Carole laughed to herself. Mrs. Reg's stories were never what she expected. People who told horse stories usually told about the unlikely undersized weakling foal who grew up to take blue ribbons at the National Horse Show. Real life, Carole knew, wasn't like that. Mrs. Reg was good at telling real-life stories about horses and riders. Her horses always had good points and bad ones the way most real-life horses did—except Cobalt. And their owners were real people, too, with good and bad mixed together.

"Come on, Mrs. Reg," Carole urged her. "Tell me. You must have had a favorite horse over all the others, didn't you?"

"Oh, let's see, now," Mrs. Reg mused. "Of course, I loved to ride Lady Day, but then I could watch a beauty like Jesse's Pride forever. What a lovely horse he was. And then, there was the jumper; Roo was what we called him, short for Kangaroo. There was a whole bunch of grays, one after the other, that Max kept for this funny old woman in town. Said she wanted horses with whiter hair than her own. And then—"

"You mean there never was a favorite?" Carole asked as she hung the final stirrup leather on the rack and tossed the bits into the bit tray.

Mrs. Reg shook her head. "Nope, never was," she said, and Carole knew she was telling the truth. Mrs. Reg loved all her horses, in one way or another.

Just then, the little black kitten succeeded in getting over the top edge of the box.

"You better catch that one!" Mrs. Reg said.

The kitten began stumbling across the tack room floor in search of adventure. He found a piece of straw and started batting it fiercely.

Carole and Mrs. Reg laughed, watching the little creature fight the straw so valiantly.

"He's something," Carole said.

"He sure is," Mrs. Reg agreed. "Let me know when you decide on a name for him, okay?"

Carole had completed putting away the sack of extra leathers, bits, and stirrups. She was done now, finished with Pine Hollow. She didn't really want to remind Mrs. Reg that she wasn't coming back.

"Okay," she said. "'Bye." Mrs. Reg told her good-night and Carole left slowly, saying good-bye to Pine Hollow, for the night, for the week, for—ever?

13

"YOU KNOW, I really miss Carole," Stevie told Lisa a week later.

"Me, too," Lisa agreed. "Even seeing her at school isn't the same thing as riding with her. She waves to me in the hall and sometimes we sit together at lunch. But she won't talk about horses! Can you imagine? We spent the entire lunch period on Tuesday talking about *history*. Maybe you should call her. She's got to change her mind and start riding again, doesn't she?"

"I sure hope so," Stevie told Lisa. "But I do call her and it's the same thing. I talked to her three times this week and she wouldn't even use the word 'horse.' I'm still pretty sure she'll get over this. I just wish she'd do it right away!"

"Me, too—then she could help us on our research project about Max!"

"I don't think I can stand another afternoon looking at the town register," Stevie groaned. "We haven't
even found the man's name, and that register has *everything* in it: land sales, building permits, birth,
death, marriage records. Let's face it, the man was in-
visible."

"Maybe he never existed," Lisa said. "Should we
consider that possibility?"

"No way—not until we've exhausted everything
else. Besides, if our Max is Max the Third, there *had*
to be a Max the First. Right?"

Lisa had to agree that it was logical. "Okay, then,
back to the library. We've been reading the *Gazette*
until it comes out of our ears. Today, instead of that,
let's look into old books on horses. Max was some kind
of star in his day—maybe he made it into the books
about horses."

"Well . . . okay. But I think there might be an
awful lot of books on horses in the library." Stevie
sighed.

Willow Creek was in the heart of Virginia's horse
country. Horses had played an important part in the
lives of its citizens for a long time. Stevie knew there
was a good chance that the library could have lots of
books about horses, breeding, records, and ownership.
She sighed again. At least she wasn't going to have to
read any more about the controversial town sewers!

"And no more Mrs. Rappaport!" she said out loud.
Lisa grinned at her. "Listen," Stevie continued, "I had
a great idea last night. Since Max almost certainly

owned some Thoroughbreds, maybe we could get some information about him from the Thoroughbred Owners and Breeders Association. They have a *million* years' worth of records about horses and owners."

"Hey, that's a great idea," Lisa told her. "I was beginning to think we'd used up all our sources. Well, congratulations! Since you had the idea, *you* get to write the letter to them while I look in the books."

The girls stepped into the library. Their newfound friend, the librarian, was at the desk, eager to help them.

"Want to look at some more newspapers?" she asked. "You know, at the turn of the century, there was a second weekly being published in town. We have some of those, too. Want to read those?"

"I don't think so," Lisa told her. "We're going to try something else first. Do you have a section on horses and breeding and ownership, that sort of thing?"

"Oh, sure we do," the librarian said. "After all, this is horse country. Come on, I'll show you."

Lisa followed the woman into the stacks while Stevie settled into a hard wooden chair in the main reading area. She hated writing letters. She especially hated writing letters to people she didn't know. And most of all, she hated writing letters when she didn't know what it was she really wanted to ask—and she was afraid that when she *did* figure out what she wanted to ask, it might sound dumb.

"Dear Sir," she wrote. She erased the comma and added "or Madam." That sounded better. She crossed that out and wrote "Dear Madam or Sir." She'd have to recopy it in ink anyway. She bit the end of her pencil, hoping that would help her think. In books and movies, people were always biting the ends of their pencils so they could think better. It didn't make Stevie think better. It just got pieces of eraser in her mouth. She picked them out carefully. Then she stared into space. Sometimes *that* helped people in books and movies. All it did for Stevie, though, was distract her.

She watched an old man come into the library. He greeted the librarian and then sat down in a comfortable chair. The librarian brought him a newspaper. It looked like something they did every day. Stevie liked that. She wondered how long the man had been coming here to read the paper. He greeted some of the people in the library as if they were old friends. He almost made a ceremony of taking out his glasses and adjusting them. He seemed to enjoy all the little steps of his ritual. She wondered if he'd enjoy writing her letter for her. It certainly wasn't going very well. All she had so far was:

I ~~was~~ We were ~~wondering~~ hoping
you ~~w~~ could help us ~~maybe~~
find out ~~something~~ some things
about ~~somebody~~ a man

It wasn't going right at all. Stevie wished she'd never thought of the idea. Maybe when Lisa got back with her books, *she* could write the letter and Stevie could look up "Regnery" and "Pine Hollow" in the indexes. While she waited, she began to draw horses on the pad in front of her.

The old man finished the first section of the paper, which he had read from front to back, and picked up the second section. He seemed to be reading a little more slowly now—almost as if he didn't want his afternoon ritual to end.

He was much more interesting than the dumb letter Stevie was supposed to write. As a matter of fact, a lot of people in the library were more interesting than that. There was a lady standing outside the door of the library with a slice of pizza in her hand. She couldn't bring it inside, so she was finishing it outside. Finally, when the lady tried to jam the rest of the slice into her mouth, a big gob of cheese slid off the pizza, down her blouse, and plopped onto the sidewalk.

Stevie clapped a hand over her mouth to stifle her giggles. She wished Lisa had seen the woman, too, so they could laugh about it together. The woman chewed the last bite and stepped into the library. Stevie thought she didn't know about the stripe of tomato sauce on her blouse. It would be hard to wash. Then the woman looked up and saw Stevie staring at her. Nervously, Stevie looked away, pretending she was interested in something going on behind her.

And suddenly, she was. Because there was Veronica diAngelo sitting at a table on the other side of a bookcase. Through the open shelves, Stevie could see that she was concentrating very hard on the book in front of her. Veronica, ever the perfect little lady, was sitting backwards in her chair, with her legs straddling the seat.

"Oh, boy, have they got books about horses here!" Lisa exclaimed, dropping a stack of books on their table.

"Shhhh!" Stevie hissed, pointing through the shelves. As soon as Lisa saw Veronica, she sat down to watch, too.

"What's she doing?" Lisa asked. "It can't be homework. Her housekeeper and her gardener and her chauffeur probably does it for her!"

"I'm surprised to see her here at all," Stevie said. "I would have thought that if she needed a library, her daddy would buy her one!"

They giggled at their jokes, but they were more than a little curious. Veronica's left arm was in a cast and in a sling. She was using it to hold a book open on the table. In her right hand was a twelve-inch ruler. There was something very familiar about the way she was straddling the chair.

"It's like she's riding!" Lisa said. Veronica was sitting as if she were on a horse, and she held the ruler as if it were a riding crop. Just then, with her eyes glued to the book, Veronica leaned forward in her chair, lifted her seat out of the chair, and brought the two back legs off the floor.

"She's jumping!" Stevie said. "Look—perfect jump position!" Veronica sat forward in the chair, leaning toward the table so she could see the book. Her seat was raised slightly from the chair and she put her weight on the balls of her feet. Her back was flat, her knees bent but supple. Suddenly, her body folded forward and her head came up.

"She's watching where she's going and keeping herself perfectly centered. Up and over—" Stevie narrated.

Slowly and smoothly, Veronica rocked herself into an upright position, bringing the rear legs of the chair back to the floor. She settled back onto the chair and relaxed.

"Well!" Stevie said. "That's better than she ever did it on a horse."

"But why here?" Lisa asked. "She's had all the lessons she could want. She had the finest horse in the stable. Why is she studying riding in the library?"

"I think you and I have just seen a side of Veronica that's never been seen before—and may never be seen again," Stevie said. "What I think is that Veronica's had a zillion lessons and a fabulous horse, but she never listened and she never learned. She thought she was too good to make a mistake, but she was wrong. She knows that now. Cobalt's life was a horrible price, but at least she learned something from it."

"You could be right," Lisa agreed. "But if I know Veronica, she'd never admit that to anybody. If we let her know we saw her, she'll tell us we were wrong. But we're not. Look, there she goes again."

While Stevie and Lisa watched, Veronica went through the jumping motions several more times, improving with each try. Finally, she seemed satisfied with her efforts and stood up from the table. Furtively, she closed the book and took it back to the shelves in the riding section where Lisa had found her stack of books. Then, as Veronica left the library, Stevie and Lisa buried themselves in books so she wouldn't recognize them. The door closed behind Veronica.

"Now, that's what I call amazing," Stevie said. But Lisa didn't hear her. She was already combing through the books she'd gotten.

"Nothing," she said, slamming another book on the reject pile. "How's your letter coming?" she asked.

"Same," Stevie said noncommittally, though actually she was pleased with her progress—on the picture of the horse she was drawing. Her letter was at zero.

Fifteen minutes later, Lisa shook her head. "There's nothing at all here. Unless we get a response to your letter, I think we're going to have to give up."

"I don't think we'll get any answer to this," Stevie confessed, shoving the sketch into her pocket. She helped Lisa carry the books back to the desk for reshelving.

"You don't look very happy," the librarian said. "Perhaps if you could tell me exactly what you're looking for, I could suggest another source?"

"I don't think so," Stevie said. But Lisa gave her a look that reminded her who the A-student was.

"Maybe," Lisa said. "If it's not too much trouble."

"That's what I'm here for," the librarian said eagerly.

"Well, we're doing a report about the men who made Willow Creek what it is today. Our subject is Maxmillian Regnery, the founder of Pine Hollow Stables. All we know is that he started the stable early this century and it doesn't look like we'll learn anything else, either. Any suggestions?"

"Max? Is that what you're after?" said a gruff male voice from behind them.

Stevie and Lisa turned. It was the white-haired man who had been reading his newspaper.

"Maxmillian Regnery the First," Lisa said.

"Old Max, Senior," the man said.

"Right, him," Stevie said. "Did you know him?" The man nodded. "Really?" she persisted.

"Said so, didn't I?" he retorted.

"Well, who was he? Where did he come from? What was he like? How did he get the money to buy the stable? Was he a real wild guy?" Stevie found herself so excited to be nearing a "source," as Lisa called it, that the questions were just bubbling out of her.

"Was he at the earthquake?" Lisa asked.

"No, it was San Juan Hill, I'm sure!" Stevie cut in.

"You girls talking about Old Max who took over that stable, right?"

"Right!" they said, breathlessly.

"Dullest man I ever knew," the old man said.

"You're kidding!" Lisa exclaimed. "He was part of the Russian Revolution, wasn't he? That's not dull."

"Nope, and it's not true, either," the man said.

Finally, they were going to get answers, and Stevie had the feeling that they were going to be surprised at what they were.

"You know, Mr., uh—"

"Thompson," the man supplied.

"Mr. Thompson, we were just going over to the coffee shop for a soda. Would you like to come with us? We could buy you a soda and you could tell us about Max the First."

"Ice-cream soda?" he asked, with a twinkle in his eyes.

"Sure," Stevie said, knowing that would deplete her allowance. But if she could learn about Max the First, it would be worth every penny—even if it meant she wasn't going to like what she heard.

"You're on," he said, and they left.

Stevie, Lisa, and Mr. Thompson settled into a back booth in the coffee shop. Stevie was careful about picking their spot. She didn't want anybody else from Pine Hollow to see them. This was a Saddle Club secret.

In a few minutes, they all had their orders and Mr. Thompson began to tell the story. Lisa and Stevie sat still, absolutely astonished. The tale was so different from what they'd expected that it *had* to be the truth.

Maxmillian Regnery I, the elderly man told them, was a rather dull, totally normal human being. He was the son of Irish immigrants who had come to America in the 1850's. Max's father was a blacksmith. Max had tried smithing, but wasn't any good at it. He'd gone to school, but hadn't done well. He'd tried working at the dry goods store, but that hadn't worked either since he wasn't very good with figures. Eventually, he'd gone to work at a stable, tending horses. He had been good at that.

The stable's owner, none other than Mr. Rappaport (Stevie liked that part), thought Max showed some potential, so he'd given him a raise of ten cents a week. Old Max had put away every penny he could— including all ten cents of his raise a week—and had bought Pine Hollow after Rappaport died. Max the First had lived his entire life in Willow Creek, and, as far as the girls could tell, had never left it—not even for the San Francisco Earthquake *or* the Russian Revolution!

"What was he really like—you know, as a person?" Stevie asked.

"I told you. He was dull. Really dull. You couldn't make conversation with the man. People who learned to ride from him—and he *was* a good rider, I remember that—used to joke about him. He was so rigid, wouldn't let anybody fiddle in his classes. You couldn't talk to the other students. He used to make a big thing, too, about talking to the horses. 'They don't speak English!' he'd yell. I was one of his students, you know. My mother, bless her, invited the man and his wife for dinner one night to discuss my riding lessons. She wanted me to learn to jump right away, but he refused. 'One year,' he said sternly. He wouldn't budge. He also wouldn't let me get out of the chores at the stable. He made all the students work like stablehands! They left right after dinner. My father swore he'd never speak to my mother again if she had Old Max back in the house. 'This is *my* house,' he said. 'And I won't be bored to death in it!' She never did invite them back. I stopped riding soon after that, too."

So that was Max the First. No hero of the earthquake, San Juan Hill, or the Russian Revolution. Just an ordinary man who was extraordinarily dull. In fact, the only interesting thing about him was that his grandson, Max the Third, taught riding exactly the same way he had, seventy-five years earlier! But Max the Third wasn't dull—far from it. His students adored him.

"What are we doing to *do*?" Lisa asked Stevie, almost desperate, after Mr. Thompson had left the coffee shop.

"Do?" Stevie echoed. "What do you mean?"

"Well, now we know Max's story, and it's not worth telling."

"We're not going to tell it," Stevie said. "But now we won't have to bother with the rumors other people started. We can start our own!" Stevie's eyes lit up. "Max was kidnapped by pirates, you know. They stole everything he owned and abandoned him on a South Sea island where the only inhabitants were horses.

When he was finally rescued by the Tasmanian Navy, he refused to leave unless he could bring some of the horses—" she said, remembering a dream she'd had on the MTO.

"That's the idea!" Lisa said enthusiastically. "Now we're in business."

They drank up the last of their sodas and headed home. On the way out of the coffee shop, Stevie dropped the scribbled and scratched draft of her letter into the garbage.

14

"HONEY, I'M GOING out now. Are you sure you don't want to come with me?" Colonel Hanson asked Carole.

"No thanks, Dad. Have a good time playing tennis. Mrs. Lerner's your partner today, huh?"

"Yes, and she's got a mean backhand!" he said. "We beat the Morrisons in straight sets last week. Tennis is a great sport. Would you like to try some lessons?"

"No, but thanks anyway," Carole said. She knew her father was trying to be helpful. It was Saturday—the day she used to go horseback riding. For the last few weeks, her father had been full of suggestions for Saturday activities. Carole hadn't wanted to do any of them. "I have to read about pyramids for my term paper. I think I'll do that today."

"After tennis, Barbara and I are going out to dinner with the Morrisons."

Carole's ears perked up. "Is that a date?" she asked.

"Well, I'm not sure I'd call it a date. It's just sort of, you know, like a—well, a date, I guess."

Carole laughed at her father's stammering. "It's okay, Dad. I like the idea of you going out on a date— even with Mrs. Lerner. As long as she doesn't use her mean backhand on you!"

"Thanks for your concern," he said, giving her a hug. "We won't be late. There's a frozen pizza in the fridge and *Sands of Iwo Jima* is on TV tonight at ten. That's the John Wayne movie about the Marines in World War Two. I'll make the popcorn this time. Is it a date?" he asked slyly.

"Well, er, uh," Carole stammered, teasing her father. "I'm not, uh, exactly, well, sure I'd call it a— er—*date*."

"Okay, then *you* make the popcorn. I'll see you later, you rascal."

"Okay, it's a date," Carole told him, grinning. She and her father loved to watch old movies together and her father was never happier than when the movies were about the Marines. That would be a fun evening to look forward to.

In the meantime, Carole was very pleased that her father was spending the day with Mrs. Lerner. He'd been talking about her a lot recently, so Carole wasn't surprised they had a date.

So, that took care of her father. But what about her?

Carole didn't want to read about pyramids. She wanted to ride Cobalt. She wanted, once more, to feel the magnificent horse beneath her, flying across a field, lofting over a jump, moving surely and gracefully, responding to her every command.

Carole put her hands over her face and shook her head, but she couldn't shake the image of Cobalt from her mind.

Then, almost without thinking, Carole stood up, went to her room and changed her clothes, got her wallet and her house keys, and left the house, locking the door behind her.

In a short time, the bus drew up to the curb where she waited. She dropped her fare into the box and found a seat at the rear of the bus. It was six stops exactly. How well she knew them! Almost blindly, she descended from the bus at the shopping center and walked across the lot, down the street, across the field. To Pine Hollow.

It was still early on Saturday. People were riding already, but the class of her own friends wouldn't ride until afternoon. Carole was pretty sure she could get into the stable without anybody seeing her. She wasn't in the mood to talk and she didn't want to answer any questions. She'd come to find answers to her own questions.

She slipped into the side door of the stable. Mrs. Reg was in the tack room, but she didn't look up as Carole passed the open door. Patch and Pepper were out of their stalls—in class or on the trails, Carole thought.

And there was the third stall, the empty one. It was Cobalt's stall. It had been cleaned out completely, with fresh straw covering the floor. The clean feed and water buckets had been turned upside down to dry the last time they had been washed, and they'd been left there. It was empty, unoccupied, waiting.

Carole slid the door open and stepped inside. She breathed deeply, loving the pungent scent of the stable. For a moment, she thought that if she closed her eyes very tight and then reopened them, maybe, just maybe, Cobalt would reappear. She shut her lids, blocking out the streams of sunlight that came through the window. When she opened her eyes again, Cobalt wasn't there. And then Carole really knew for the first time that Cobalt was gone and he wasn't going to come back. No amount of wishing would change that, ever.

She leaned against the wall of the stall and slid down to sit on the clean straw. Then, for the first time since Cobalt had died, Carole cried. She sat there alone in his empty stall, her body racked with sorrow. Tears streamed down her face in silent anguish.

When all her tears were spent, she lay down in the straw and slept, exhausted by her grief.

Carole didn't know how long she slept. When she awoke, the sun was no longer coming in the window. That meant it had to be afternoon, but she didn't know what time in the afternoon. For a moment, she wondered what had awakened her, and then she heard the voices.

"No, Daddy, *no!*" the girl's voice whined. It was Veronica. Carole hated the idea that Veronica might find her in Cobalt's stall. She shifted from the side of the stall, cowering against the front wall where she couldn't be seen by somebody walking by. But she could hear everything.

"You're being silly, Ronnie," a man said. Carole realized that was Mr. diAngelo. It was a little surprising to hear him call her Ronnie. Veronica certainly wouldn't let anybody else call her that!

"Daddy, the answer is no, and I mean it."

Were Stevie and Lisa wrong? Was Veronica giving up riding, too? Was that what she was fighting with her father about?

"Delilah's a good horse!" Mr. diAngelo said. "Isn't she the mare that girl—what's her name, Carole?—rides?"

"Yes, Daddy. Carole used to ride Delilah. She's stopped coming to lessons, though."

"If Carole was the best rider in your class, then I'm sure Max gave her the best horse in the stable. And, pet, you'd look so good on her—she's got that beautiful creamy mane and the golden coat. . . ."

"That's not the point, Daddy."

"Well, if Delilah's not the right horse, I'll have my agent buy you another Thoroughbred at the auction next month. We got enough out of the insurance for Cobalt to buy you the best horse at the sale. You want one that looks like Cobalt?"

"Daddy, what a horse looks like doesn't matter," Veronica said, echoing the thought in Carole's mind.

"It's how a horse rides that's important. But even more important is how the *rider* rides."

"What are you saying, Veronica?" the man asked his daughter.

There was a long silence. Carole held her breath, waiting for Veronica's answer.

"It was my fault, Daddy," she said at last. "I caused the accident that broke my arm and that killed Cobalt."

"Nonsense!" her father protested. "You said it was Max's fault. He shouldn't have set up the jump the way he did."

"I was wrong," Veronica said. "It was a tricky jump, all right, but Max had told us how to jump it, and I decided not to pay any attention to him. If I'd had any sense, I would have told him I didn't know how to make that jump. Cobalt would never have refused the jump. But I went ahead anyway. And it cost Cobalt his life."

"Oh, don't worry about that, lamb," Mr. diAngelo said, comforting his daughter. "After all, we got the insurance money, didn't we?"

"Money doesn't have anything to do with it, Daddy! Cobalt's dead—and I don't want to own another horse until I can take care of him!"

As long as Carole had known Veronica, she'd never heard her admit that she'd made a mistake. In this case, Veronica was absolutely right. She wasn't a very good rider. She didn't deserve a horse like Cobalt.

She didn't listen to instructions. Her carelessness had
cost Cobalt his life. Carole shook her head in wonder.
She never would have thought that those were lessons
Veronica could learn. Now, not only had she learned
them, but she was trying, without success, to teach
them to her father.

"You don't have to worry about taking care of your
horse, Ronnie," her father said, completely missing his
daughter's point. "That's why Max has all these stableboys here. *They* can take care of him for you."

"But they can't ride him for me, Daddy," she said.
"Thanks for wanting to buy me a horse, but I'll keep
on riding the stable horses until I've learned a lot more
about riding. One day I'll own another horse. But not
until I'm ready."

"I can just see you on that pretty palomino, Ronnie," Mr. diAngelo said, his voice dripping with temp-
tation.

"*Daddy!*" Veronica said.

Stunned, Carole remained hidden in Cobalt's
empty stall.

15

"I CAN DO it," Carole said to the empty stall, after Veronica's footsteps had faded away. "And even more important, I want to do it."

In a rush, all of her dreams came back to her. For as long as she could remember, her love of horses had been the one thing in Carole's life that had never changed. With her father in the Marines, she'd spent much of her life moving from one base to another, or living alone with her mother while her father had duty someplace they couldn't live. Her mother sometimes used to joke that they ought to "take up residence" in a moving van. But Carole hadn't minded, because wherever they lived, there were always horses.

She'd first learned to ride at the stables on the bases. When the bases didn't have stables, her parents always found a stable nearby. Then she'd found that taking classes at a private stable was a good way to make friends in a new town. Pine Hollow was the best of all, too. Max always had really good horses and he was a strict but good teacher. Max and his father and grandfather had trained quite a lot of national championship riders—and even a few Olympic riders.

Her whole life, all Carole had ever wanted to do was to ride horses, own them, breed them, train them. And yet, she had been willing to give it all up just because of Cobalt.

Now she knew that she couldn't give up on her dreams, but maybe it wasn't going to be so easy to make them come true. After all, she'd just about walked out on Max and Mrs. Reg. Max wouldn't take just anybody as a student and he required a real devotion from his riders. Carole realized that it was possible Max would tell her she wasn't welcome.

"Well, there's only one way to find out, isn't there?" she asked herself.

She stood up in the stall and brushed the straw off of her blouse. She was more than a little surprised, when she looked down, to see that she was wearing her breeches and riding boots. With a start, she understood that she'd made up her mind to ride again the moment she'd decided to come to the stable that morning. Without realizing it at all, she'd changed into her riding clothes!

She swept the straw off her breeches, plucked a final strand out of her hair, and peered over the stall door. Until she had talked to Max—and until she'd ridden again and proved to herself that she could still do it with the same commitment—she really didn't want to talk to anybody or answer anybody's questions. Fortunately, the coast was clear.

Carole stepped out into the aisle and headed for Max's office. But as she passed the tack room she saw Mrs. Reg. Mrs. Reg didn't see her, though. She was entirely too busy retrieving a little black kitten from a rafter in the tack room.

"You get down here, you rascal. How did you get up there?" she demanded furiously. Mrs. Reg stood on a chair and reached for the kitten, but he scampered along the rafter, just out of her reach.

"I'll give you a hand, Mrs. Reg," Carole said, stepping into the tack room. "You shouldn't be standing on a chair with your arthritis," she added.

"Oh, I wouldn't, believe me, if I didn't have to get this little one down. Remember him? This is the cute little newborn kitten you were playing with. Now, he's a devil—an absolute devil. He's into everything."

"Listen, you stay on the chair there, and I'll shoo him back to you, okay?"

"A devil! That's what this one is," Mrs. Reg continued, barely acknowledging Carole's presence. "Whatever you expect him to do, he doesn't. Now, you try shooing him, okay?"

Carole moved a tack box under the rafter and climbed up on it. The kitten was trapped between Carole and Mrs. Reg. Eventually, he'd get to one of them.

"Here, kitty," Mrs. Reg invited.

"Go on! Shoo!" Carole said, hustling the black fur-ball toward Mrs. Reg.

With that, the kitten turned from Mrs. Reg and began walking precisely toward Carole. His little tail waved back and forth to preserve his balance. "You're right about him," Carole said. "He does just the opposite of what an ordinary cat would do, doesn't he?"

"Since the day he was born," Mrs. Reg agreed.

"Go away, kitty!" Carole said, looking straight into his sky-blue eyes. "Go away!"

She could hear his purring, the magical motor going full tilt. The little kitten stepped off the rafter and onto Carole's shoulder. Cradling him so that he wouldn't fall, Carole stepped off the tack box and then helped Mrs. Reg get off her chair.

"Got a name for him yet?" Mrs. Reg asked, picking up their conversation from several weeks ago, just as if no time had passed at all.

"Yeah, I do," Carole said. She sat down on the tack box and held the kitten on her lap. Within seconds, the black kitten's purring stopped. He was curled up and sound asleep.

"His name's Snowball," Carole told Mrs. Reg.

"Perfect!" Mrs. Reg said, laughing. "He's so contrary that he's truly earned a name like that. But there's a problem with that."

"What's that?" Carole asked, stroking the kitten softly.

"Our cats are named after horses. I don't know of any 'Snowball.'"

"Can't you make an exception?"

"I don't think so," Mrs. Reg said. "But I have another solution. If he's not a stable cat, he doesn't have to have a stable name. Why don't you keep him? He'll be weaned and ready to go to a new home in about two weeks. If you'd like him, ask your dad, okay?"

"Okay," Carole said. "I'd like that."

She picked up the sleeping kitten and put him back in the box where he'd been born. All his littermates were awake from their naps and were crawling out of the box.

"I'll ask Dad tonight," Carole said, sure that he'd agree. After all, who could resist a little black kitten named Snowball?

"Snowball's the right name, that's for sure," Mrs. Reg said.

Then Carole remembered that she'd once thought she should name the kitten Cobalt. That wouldn't have been right at all. Cobalt *was* a great horse, but the kitten deserved his own name. Carole glanced at the clock in the tack room. Only fifteen minutes until class!

"Gotta see Max!" she said. "'Bye!"

She ran out of the tack room and headed for Max's office, skidding to a stop as she neared the door. Then she proceeded to walk calmly. It wouldn't do to arrive huffing and puffing.

"Can I talk to you, Max?" she asked politely.

"Sure, Carole. Come on in," he said, smiling warmly. Carole hoped he meant it.

"Max, I was wondering if it would be okay for me to come back—join the class again."

Max was quiet for a minute. Was he angry with her? Had he filled her spot in the class? Did he have rules about quitters? Was she going to have to find another stable?

"Carole," he began, "I know what you've been through. I know how much you cared for Cobalt and I know how much his death hurt you—as indeed it did all of us. I am very happy to have you back. But class starts in fifteen—" he glanced at his digital watch "—thirteen minutes. Can you get saddled up by then?"

"You bet I can!" she said. "I'll get Delilah's saddle and bridle right away."

"Not Delilah," Max said.

Carole gulped. If she couldn't ride Delilah, that must mean that Mr. diAngelo had talked Veronica into letting him buy the horse! That meant that Veronica hadn't learned anything after all. Would she kill Delilah, too?

"I guess you had to do it," Carole said dully. She understood that the owner of a stable really had to go along with some of the patrons. After all, Mr. diAngelo owned the bank and he could cause trouble for Max—

"Had to do what?" he asked.

"Had to sell her," Carole said. "I heard that Mr. diAngelo wanted to buy her for Veronica. I understand that kind of thing happens." She was trying to be realistic.

"Not to me, it doesn't," Max said, surprising her. "I couldn't sell her now, anyway."

"Is she sick?" Carole asked, suddenly recalling how oddly Delilah had behaved on the MTO with her mood shifts and unpredictable appetite.

"Not exactly," Max said evasively.

"Then what, exactly?" Carole said.

"She's carrying a foal, Carole. She's due in a couple of months and until then she'll have rest and pasture time. Nobody rides her and she's not for sale."

A foal! That meant there would be a birth at the stable. It could be a beautiful palomino like Delilah—a whole new life coming to Pine Hollow.

"You mean she wasn't sick on the MTO?"

"Nope, she was just getting ready for motherhood—and sometimes mares act up a bit when their time gets nearer. She's fine and healthy. So's the foal so far. Vet says she'll be delivering at the end of the summer. So, it's time for her to stop work."

"That's wonderful!" Carole sat still in the chair across from Max's desk, too excited to move, or even to think about class.

"Carole," Max said gently. She looked up at him. "You haven't asked the question I was expecting."

"What's that?"

"You haven't asked who the sire of Delilah's foal is."

"Okay, who is—" Carole suddenly didn't have to ask. There was only one stallion at Pine Hollow, only one horse who *could* have sired a foal. "Cobalt?"

Max smiled and nodded. "See, in a way, he's going to live on." Carole was silent, taking in the good news.

Suddenly Max was his old businesslike self again. "Breeding a mare is a lot of work, Carole," he said. "From now on, we're going to have to watch Delilah carefully. We want a healthy foal. And after it's born, there's going to be even more work. We'll be doing feeding and tending and training—" he paused and looked into Carole's eyes. "You'll help, won't you?"

"*Will* I!" she said breathlessly. It was a dream come true.

"Okay, if you're going to help, you're going to have to be a better rider than you are now. What are you doing just sitting here? Why aren't you getting ready for class? You're to ride Diablo from now on, understand?"

"Yes, *sir*!" she said. She stood up and saluted Max, Marine Corps-style—just like her father taught her.

And then she floated on air back out to the stable. She didn't have a second to waste before class.

"Hi, Carole!" Betsy Cavanaugh greeted her as she tried to dash down the aisle to Diablo's stall. "Did you hear?"

"Hear what?" Carole asked suspiciously. She didn't think Max had shared the news about Delilah yet, otherwise she was certain Lisa or Stevie would have called to tell her.

"About Max—the First. He was captured by pirates!"

"Give me a break," Carole said, making her way to her horse.

"No, it's true! I think it is, anyway," Betsy said.

Carole didn't have time to listen to any more. She stepped into Diablo's stall and began putting the saddle on him.

"Max the First was a horse thief," a voice told her, coming over the door to the stall. It was Meg Durham speaking. "It seems that he rode with Billy the Kid and they were rustling horses out west. Then—"

"Meg! I'm late for class and I have to get this done in a hurry. Tell me about it after class, maybe?"

"Sure, Carole," Meg said. "Nice to see you back."

By the time Carole had the saddle and bridle on Diablo and was walking him toward the ring—and toward the good-luck horseshoe—two other people had told her two other stories about Max the First. Carole had never heard such zany stories in her whole life— and every single person who told her a tale swore it was true.

"Carole! You're back!" Stevie shrieked. She had just mounted Comanche and was walking around the ring until class started.

Lisa came up behind her on Pepper. "Oh, Carole, I knew you'd come back. I'm so glad to see you. We missed you!"

"Really?" Carole brushed the good-luck horseshoe with her right hand and then mounted Diablo. "And I think I got back just in time to see this place go crazy. What's all this stuff I hear about Max the First?"

Lisa and Stevie exchanged glances and then slapped their hands over their mouths. Carole had the distinct impression they were trying to stifle giggles.

"Are you going to tell me that Max was actually the first human being to reach the south pole—on horseback? A little-known expedition that took place at the turn of the century?"

"Hey, that's a great idea!" Stevie said, her eyes popping open.

"What is going on around here?" Carole asked.

But before either Lisa or Stevie could answer, Max entered the ring.

"Now, class begins!" he said sternly. From that moment on, talking was strictly forbidden.

"Saddle Club meeting at TD's after class!" Stevie hissed.

Carole nodded happily. Did she have news for them!

"SO YOU GUYS found this old guy at the library who actually knew Max?" Carole asked in surprise.

The three girls were seated at their favorite table in TD's, the ice cream store at the shopping center. They were each working their way through a sundae, the first Stevie had been able to afford since buying Mr. Thompson the soda!

"Oh, yeah!" Stevie said. "And Max was nothing like anyone had guessed! He was a good rider and a strict teacher—just like our Max—but apparently he was this boring old guy who could put people practically to sleep just by talking. He never left Willow Creek his whole life. He never even did anything *interesting,* so forget about exciting."

"So, why's everybody telling me about pirates and expeditions and everything?"

"See, now that we know the truth, we don't have to worry about anybody believing it!" Lisa said. "So, we tell people we've done research—and that part's true—and this is what we found. Only we tell everybody something different *and* we tell them not to tell anybody else!"

"Somehow this sounds like an idea of Stevie's," Carole said, laughing. "You're really something, you know?"

"I never could have done it without Lisa," Stevie said. "She had a lot of great research ideas. But if you ever get curious about a certain Mrs. Rappaport, or the town sewer system, just ask me, okay?"

"You'll be the first person I'll ask," Carole assured her. "What I really want to ask, though, is what's going on with Veronica?" Carole told them about the conversation Veronica had with her father. Stevie and Lisa told her about Veronica's jumping class—in the library. "Is she changing—or what?" Carole asked.

"I think she is," Lisa said solemnly. "She really learned something when Cobalt got hurt. You have to respect that, don't you?"

"I respect it," Stevie said. "But it doesn't make me like her much better. She's still a pain. Now, if she stops being a *pain*, that'll be news!" The Saddle Club members laughed together.

"Now, let me tell you *my* news." Stevie and Lisa listened eagerly, almost as thrilled as Carole when she told them about Snowball and then, best of all, about Delilah's foal.

"I can't wait!" Stevie exclaimed. "The newborns are *so* cute! Do you think it'll be black like Cobalt—or a pretty palomino like Delilah?"

They talked animatedly about the foal for a while as they finished their sundaes. Then the talk turned to Carole. She'd known it would come, and she knew that her friends deserved an answer.

"What made you decide to come back?" Lisa asked.

"There were a lot of things. I think that you were right in a way when you said I was horse shy. But not just about any horse—it was Cobalt. It hurt so much when he died that I was afraid I might get hurt again if something like that happened to another horse. But when I saw what Veronica had learned—well, I thought if there's hope for her, then there's hope for me. Anyway, the only thing worse than losing something you care about is not having something you care about at all. I learned that when Mom died."

Stevie and Lisa sat quietly. "There was something else," Carole continued. "I finally realized that no matter how much I cared about him, Cobalt wasn't mine. He belonged to somebody else."

"But you rode him more than Veronica did!" Lisa reminded her.

"I did, that's right. And I rode him better. But Mrs. Reg had the final lesson for me, though she didn't say it in so many words. There are lots of horses, some good, some bad, most mixes of good and bad. And I want to ride them all!"

"Uh-oh," Stevie said. Carole and Lisa turned to her. "With that kind of determination, Carole won't be horse shy anymore, that's for sure. But the poor horses—they'll become Carole shy!"

The three girls laughed together and it felt very, very good. The Saddle Club was now back in full operation.

ABOUT THE AUTHOR

BONNIE BRYANT is the author of more than fifty books for young readers, including novelizations of movie hits such as *Teenage Mutant Ninja Turtles* and *Honey, I Blew Up the Kid,* written under her married name, B. B. Hiller.

Ms. Bryant began writing The Saddle Club in 1986. Although she had done some riding before that, she intensified her studies then and found herself learning right along with her characters Stevie, Carole, and Lisa. She claims that they are all much better riders than she is.

Ms. Bryant was born and raised in New York City. She lives in Greenwich Village with her two sons.

THE SADDLE CLUB

A blue-ribbon series by Bonnie Bryant

Stevie, Carole and Lisa are all very different, but they *love* horses! The three girls are best friends at Pine Hollow Stables, where they ride and care for all kinds of horses. Come to Pine Hollow and get ready for all the fun and adventure that comes with being 13!

From Bantam-Skylark Books
IT'S

From Betsy Haynes, the bestselling author of the Taffy Sinclair books, comes
THE FABULOUS FIVE. Follow the adventures of Jana Morgan and the rest of
THE FABULOUS FIVE in Wakeman Jr. High.

☐	SEVENTH-GRADE RUMORS (Book #1)	15625-X	$2.95
☐	THE TROUBLE WITH FLIRTING (Book #2)	15633-0	$2.95
☐	THE POPULARITY TRAP (Book #3)	15634-9	$2.95
☐	HER HONOR, KATIE SHANNON (Book #4)	15640-3	$2.95
☐	THE BRAGGING WAR (Book #5)	15651-9	$2.75
☐	THE PARENT GAME (Book #6)	15670-5	$2.75
☐	THE KISSING DISASTER (Book #7)	15710-8	$2.75
☐	THE RUNAWAY CRISIS (Book #8)	15719-1	$2.75
☐	THE BOYFRIEND DILEMMA (Book #9)	15720-5	$2.75
☐	PLAYING THE PART (Book #10)	15745-0	$2.75
☐	HIT AND RUN (Book #11)	15746-9	$2.75
☐	KATIE'S DATING TIPS (Book #12)	15748-5	$2.75
☐	THE CHRISTMAS COUNTDOWN (Book #13)	15756-6	$2.75
☐	SEVENTH-GRADE MENACE (Book #14)	15763-9	$2.75
☐	MELANIE'S IDENTITY CRISIS (Book #15)	15775-2	$2.75
☐	THE HOT-LINE EMERGENCY (Book #16)	15781-7	$2.99
☐	CELEBRITY AUCTION (Book #17)	15784-1	$2.75
☐	TEEN TAXI (Book #18)	15794-9	$2.75
☐	THE BOYS-ONLY CLUB (Book #19)	15809-0	$2.95
☐	THE WITCHES OF WAKEMAN (Book #20)	15830-9	$2.75
☐	JANA TO THE RESCUE (Book #21)	15840-6	$2.75
☐	MELANIE'S VALENTINE (Book #22)	15845-7	$2.95
☐	MALL MANIA (Book #23)	15052-X	$2.95
☐	THE GREAT TV TURNOFF (Book #24)	15861-7	$2.95
☐	THE FABULOUS FIVE MINUS ONE (Book #25)	15867-8	$2.99
☐	LAURA'S SECRET (Book #26)	15871-6	$2.99
☐	THE SCAPEGOAT (Book #27)	15872-4	$2.99
☐	BREAKING UP (Book #28)	15873-2	$2.99
☐	MELANIE EDWARDS, SUPER KISSER (Book #29)	15874-0	$2.99
☐	SIBLING RIVALRY (Book #30)	15875-9	$2.99
☐	THE FABULOUS FIVE TOGETHER AGAIN (Book #31)	15968-2	$2.99
☐	CLASS TRIP CALAMITY (Book #32)	15969-0	$2.99
☐	SUPER EDITION #1 THE FABULOUS FIVE IN TROUBLE	15814-7	$2.95
☐	SUPER EDITION #2 CARIBBEAN ADVENTURE	15831-7	$2.95
☐	SUPER EDITION #3 MISSING YOU	15876-7	$2.99
☐	SUPER EDITION #4 YEARBOOK MEMORIES	15975-5	$3.50

Buy them at your local bookstore or use this page to order:

Bantam Books, Dept. SK28, 2451 S. Wolf Road, Des Plaines, IL 60018

Please send me the items I have checked above. I am enclosing $_____
(please add $2.50 to cover postage and handling). Send check or money
order, no cash or C.O.D.s please.

Mr/Ms _____

Address _____

City/State _____ Zip _____

SK28-8/92

Please allow four to six weeks for delivery
Prices and availability subject to change without notice.